COCAINE

CONTENTS

PROSA

GEDICHTE

INTRODUCTION

To this day, the German poet and writer Walter Rheiner remains virtually unknown in the English-speaking world, despite a small but remarkable oeuvre which explores typical Expressionist themes – including metropolitan estrangement, intoxication and the horrors of trench warfare – in a manner as daring and poignant as the work of better known contemporaries such as Trakl or Heym.

Rheiner was born in Cologne as Walter Schnorrenberg on 18 March 1895.[1] His father, a traveling salesman, died in 1911 when the son was sixteen and in the midst of preparing for his final examinations at the Oberrealschule (a secondary school comparable to the Gymnasium). Without the father's income, the remaining family – Rheiner, his mother and sister – began to struggle financially. Unable to afford university, Rheiner would spend the next year or so working short apprenticeships, first at a bank in Cologne, then for an arms and munitions factory in the Belgian town of Liège, and subsequently in Paris, where he worked for a grain trading firm called Dreyfus and Co.

In the French capital, at the age of 17, he begins writing his first prose sketches, one of which, 'Miramée', is included here. A nightmarish, surreal account of a one-night stand, the short piece betrays an imagination deeply stirred by both the splendour and sleaze of the metropolitan experience. This two-sided fascination (awe and terror) with life in the big city – a typical Expressionist obsession to begin with – would become the theme to which Rheiner returned time and again in both poetry and prose. In line with the shock effect first described in Georg Simmel's essay 'The Metropolis and Mental Life' (1903), Rheiner's work portrays a dehumanizing, impersonal and machine-like city, its frantic pace and overstimulation of the senses provoking a permanent state of anxiety in its inhabitants, alienated individuals driven to addiction, madness and despair.

In 1914 Rheiner goes abroad once more, to London this time, to work at a bank. Several months later, in the summer, he is called back to Berlin to report for the military examination. The duration of his stay here is unknown, but it is long enough for the aspiring poet to strike up acquaintances with some of the leading figures of the artistic avant-garde that gather in the Café des Westens on the corner of Kurfürstendamm and Joachimsthalerstrasse. In particular, he befriends the author Johannes R. Becher, who introduces him to a scheme designed to exempt both writers from active service: they will pose as drug addicts and be declared unfit. Rheiner signs up for the experiment, but this will prove to be a fatal decision. Not only does the plan fail in its primary objective, but for Rheiner a lifelong addiction to cocaine and, later, morphine will ensue.

In 1915, Rheiner succeeds in having 'Miramée' published in *Die Aktion*.[2] The same year, he is enlisted and sent off to the Eastern Front. In 1916, he is temporarily dismissed and consigned to a hospital in Lindenburg for a detoxification cure. After the treatment he is sent back to war, but when his name is discovered on the client list of a Berlin morphine dealer, he is put on trial for sabotaging his military duty. Pending the trial, Rheiner is jailed in the town of Küstrin but eventually – apparently after having successfully defended himself – he wins the case and is released and dismissed from the army. During his time in Küstrin, he worked on several prose pieces, including 'Three Fragments from a War Novella' and 'The Death of the Dreamer Gautier Fémin' (both included here). While there are no surviving letters or diary entries that describe Rheiner's war experiences, the war 'Fragments' – whose gruesome directness reads like a literary rendering of the work of Otto Dix – provide us with unsettling glimpses:

> Waves of earth boil, hill-bubbles burst. It undulates. The grenades rise like geysers. They appear to come from the belly of the earth. Suddenly they hit in even beats. *Danse macabre!* Shrapnel sprays apart; all eyes stare up [...] Olaf thrusts, runs down, thrusts, shoots with his revolver. A blow to his shoulder. A grenade tears through a group of comrades. One of them falls into his arms, the neck-stump gurgles hot blood into his face.

In March of 1917, Rheiner returns to Cologne for a short period and meets the woman who will become the love of his life, Amalie Friederike Olle (or 'Fo', as he would refer to her), a brunette of Jewish descent of whom his mother disapproves. In June, Rheiner sets out for Berlin and Fo follows him three months later. They marry in February 1918 and the following August their first child is born, a daughter they call Renée Beate. The intensity of Rheiner's attachment is expressed by the great number of poems devoted to or inspired by Fo;

even more strikingly, his very last publication, a collection of poetry entitled *Das Fo-Buch*, would appear a good two years after their divorce, in 1921.

In October 1917, Rheiner joins the 'Expressionist Workers' Community Dresden' during an event at Dresden's Arnold gallery, to which he is invited by the young painter Conrad Felixmüller. He reads out his poetry and receives praise from the great poet Theodor Däubler, who is among the audience. Another author present at the event is Felix Stiemer, who shortly thereafter establishes the Dresdner Verlag von 1917, the publishing house that will issue most of Rheiner's future output. Within a year and a half an impressive body of work appears: 5 volumes of poetry, the novella *Cocaine* (included here), as well as numerous reviews and poems in journals like *Die Flöte*, *Die Aktion* and *Die weissen Blätter*. Rheiner now lives the bohemian life and is a regular at the Romanisches Café on Breitscheidplatz, which has replaced Des Westens as the favourite haunt of the avant-garde.

The café on Breitscheidplatz features in a particularly bloodcurdling scene in *Cocaine*, the short novella which details the demise of Tobias, a cocaine addict shooting up in the doorways and public toilets of Berlin until he finally descends into a drug-induced psychosis where streetlamps dazzle, buildings rise up through the fog like fists and residential corridors are haunted by ghostly voices.

More than just the story of an addict, *Cocaine* can be taken as a psycho-geographical mapping of Berlin's Westend, the decadent centre of Expressionism. The journey made by Tobias can easily be traced even today. Starting off at evening fall, he leaves his rented room in the 'the infinitely long street' named after 'that great philosopher whose works he'd once read and who appeared to him in the image of a cane-wielding father' (i.e. Kantstrasse), then passes under the railway bridge and emerges onto Breitscheidplatz to be dwarfed by the towering spire of the (then still intact) Gedächtniskirche. After obtaining his drugs from a nearby pharmacy, he enters the Romanisches Café (today replaced by the Europa building) and shoots up twice in the toilet. The effect of the drug is treacherous, at first euphoric but nerve-wrecking only moments later:

> Swinging over to the shiny marble table, he sat himself down between the chattering women and men. He ordered and lit one of the tangy cigarettes that were his companions in sorrow and joy.
>
> But when he looked up through the aromatic smoke pouring from his mouth, *he could see the menacing night – that night, his night, shattering these short minutes of serene rush with its black fist*, advancing inexorably with a dark, agonising new intoxication, *the endlessly stretched out rhapsody of which would torture his ears from here on.*

Fleeing in paranoia, Tobias is spat out by the revolving door and hastens along Joachimsthalerstrasse to Zoo station, where he locks himself up in one of the toilets for another round of injections. Back outside he first hides under an overpass, then walks back along the same street and ultimately ends up on Kaiserallee (presently Bundesallee), down which he continues until he reaches the Wilhelmsdorf-Friedenau railway station, about a 4-kilometre walk in total. Here he veers off and arrives in an area of recently built houses on the edge of town, where he will spend the night in the atelier of his friend Marian.

In December 1918, Rheiner and Fo decide to move to Dresden, which at first seems a move that will improve their living standards. Rheiner obtains the position of editor of the journal *Menschen*, created earlier that year by Stiemer as a political-literary platform. It is the most politically engaged periodical to come out of Dresden and the one with the most impact nationwide, with firm ties to the *Novembergruppe*, Berlin's own radical artists' collective. One of Rheiner's first contributions to the journal in January 1919, is to soundly denounce the murder of Rosa Luxemburg and Karl Liebknecht on the front page: 'They were the only ones who held the flag of revolution high these four years [...] The government is guilty of multifarious murders ... honour and glory to their slain opponents. Explain! Speak! Talk! Shout!'[3]

During this time in Dresden, Rheiner maintains friendship with Felixmüller, but also with Iwan and Claire Goll and the painter Otto Freundlich among others. He attends the Expressionist soirées Felixmüller organises in his atelier and makes an impression by reading out his poetry, 'almost crying his words'.[4] However, the editing job does not make enough money to sustain the young family, let alone Rheiner's ever increasing appetite for narcotics. He starts writing begging letters, borrows money from friends and falsifies his CV, everything to feed his addiction. To make matters worse he also switches from cocaine to morphine. When in February 1920 a son is born (Johannes Walter Karol), the family's poverty quickly becomes so acute that in May of the following year Fo is forced to move back to her mother in Cologne, taking along her daughter, while the boy is temporarily sent to an orphanage in Berlin. Rheiner begins traveling around Germany in search of work, initiating a long period of wandering that will last until January 1923, when he returns to Cologne to live with his mother.

In the autumn of 1924 Rheiner's mother forces him to go into rehab in Bonn, where he stays for half a year. In the meantime, a desperate Fo has decided to divorce him. Out of rehab, Rheiner returns to Berlin almost at once, in a last bid to find work and turn his life around. Some two months later, on the 12th of June 1925, he is found dead from an overdose of morphine in a doss-house in Kantstrasse, a stone's throw from the cafés where he had made such a promising start in the literary field eleven years earlier.

Rheiner was buried at the Kaiser-Wilhelm-Gedächtnis-Friedhof in Berlin. According to Ralph Bei, the curator of the exhibition 'Gesamtkunstwerk Expressionism' held in Darmstadt in 2010, the death of Rheiner marked the end of the era of Expressionism.[5] The times had changed decisively: that same year the new style in painting was showcased with the 'Neue Sachlichkeit' ('new objectivity') exhibition, and the first volume of *Mein Kampf* would be published. Fo left Germany for the United States in 1926, not to return until 1948. Once back in Berlin after the war, she took up work as a translator for the American forces. Some time thereafter she had a tombstone made that still marks the grave of her estranged husband today.

NOTES

1. This introduction is largely based on the following sources: Walter Rheiner, *Kokain: Lyrik, Prosa, Briefe*, ed. by Thomas Rietzschel (Leipzig: Philip Reclam, 1985); *Walter Rheiner: 1895-1925*, ed. Walter Huder, exhibition catalogue (Berlin: Akademie der Künste, 1969); the Walter Rheiner Archive at the Akademie der Künste, Berlin.

2. *Die Aktion*, year 5 (1915), 20/21. The piece would be republished three years later in the collection *Der Bunte Tag*, and then received generous praise from Iwan Goll.

3. As translated by Kathleen Chapman, 'Dresden: Collectivity is Dead: Long Live Mankind', in: *The Oxford Critical and Cultural History of Modernist Magazines*, Volume III, Europe: 1880-1940, Part 1, ed. Peter Brooke et al. (Oxford: Oxford UP, 2013), pp. 888-904.

4. Felixmüller's words, as reported in Hans-Jürgen Sarfert, 'Berlin und Dresden: Skizze der Kommunikationsbeziehungen 1909 bis 1918', in: *Literarisches Leben in Berlin*, I (Berlin: Akademie Verlag, 1987), p. 383.

5. *Gesamtkunstwerk Expressionismus*, gen. ed. Ralph Beil, catalogue for the exhibition 'Gesamkunstwerk Expressionismus: Kunst, Film, Theater, Tanz und Architektur 1905-1925', at the Matildenhöhe institute in Darmstadt, 2010 (Ostfildern: Hatje Cantz Verlag, 2010), cf. p.18, note 1.

COCAINE

COCAINE

C'est la Mort qui console, hélas! et qui fait vivre;
C'est le but de la vie, et c'est le seul espoir
Qui, comme un élixir, nous monte et nous enivre,
Et nous donne le coeur de marcher jusqu'au soir;
À travers la tempête, et la neige, et le givre,
C'est la clarté vibrante à notre horizon noir
C'est l'auberge fameuse inscrite sur le livre,
Où l'on pourra manger, et dormir, et s'asseoir;
C'est un Ange qui tient dans ses doigts magnétiques
Le sommeil et le don des rêves extatiques,
Et qui refait le lit des gens pauvres et nus;
C'est la gloire des Dieux, c'est le grenier mystique,
C'est la bourse du pauvre et sa patrie antique,
C'est le portique ouvert sur les Cieux inconnus!

BAUDELAIRE: LA MORT DES PAUVRES

I

Night draped the trees that lined the avenue, dripping down upon Tobias' shoulders as he made his way beneath the whispering branches. On and on he went, pacing up and down the street; it had been nearly two hours now.

The street clock – that ghost of bronze at the intersection – already told half-past ten. While the summer evening was dying away slowly, dissolving in the most delicate of shades behind the giant hull of the eternally grey Memorial Church, Tobias had gone out, overcome by the gloomy anxiety that always returned and only ever worsened as soon as he tried to escape or kill it in the noisy bustle of the café, that miserable place with the red velvet seats and its smirking, cold-blooded guests who lived out their surreal lives there; lives as brightly-coloured as the transfers one was given as a child. As so often before, he was headed there now, to flee the mellow summer sun that was fading away in the low skies, threatening to turn his anxiety into madness.

But the anxiety always got the better of him, and made him loathe every place he could think of – his furnished room as much as the café, or the wide-open spaces of the streets and squares. He'd left feeling agitated, with the dark evening current pouring out in blue over the heads of the passers-by. Now night had arrived. The asphalt flickered when a car rushed past, hissing at Tobias. Sweet music drifting from the café terraces engulfed him and scraps of conversation he couldn't quite make out came floating by. He found himself amidst a constant stream of colourful, distinguished ladies and discreet gentlemen, a ceaseless flow of laughing carriages and cars: the bittersweet evening song of a dark metropolis that understood how to live in its own way.

And what of him? Did he know how to live? What sort of a life was it he lived? He stood on the entrance to the square, dazed by the fountain of light and sound that surrounded him, and he pondered, briefly, abruptly: certainly not this kind of life, which was just as superficial as the bright-coloured robes, the shiny cars and smiling masks that were passing him by. So, how did he live?

What did it amount to, his getting up at ten or eleven in the morning, often even at noon, full of loathing for his lodgings, for his books, his clothes, for his own person? The daily realisation he had no money, the problem of how to obtain it – from whichever acquaintance or stranger, and by whatever means; the hunger that confronted him first thing in the morning, he despised it; his daily squabble with the old landlady demanding her rent, before he'd listlessly leave the house that revolted him as much as the infinitely long street it stood on, which carried the sneering name of that great philosopher whose works he'd once read and who appeared to him in the image of a cane-wielding father;[1] the guilty conscience with which he had to beg for money in the café or before the desks of startled editors who would blow their cigar smoke into his face and angrily tell him off; this stupidity, this horrible resentment he detected caused him to feel wronged by anyone with a decent suit, a contented appearance and a calm composure. Then the accursed night would arrive, which made him nervous and triggered this demonic anxiety that set him spinning like a whirligig. *The birds were whistling* – and he faced his inescapable fate as it materialised in front of him and ushered him along with a mighty hand: Go forth!

So on he went, from one day to the next. The day before yesterday, yesterday and today: *there was no escape*. Well, death eventually, or perhaps – *hopefully* – sooner or later something would befall him. He walked on, until … Yes, there it was! As always, he was rooted on the spot.

Night bell for the pharmacy. He rang and waited.

The light came on, and the little hatchway was opened. The pharmacist stuck out his bald head.

'Doctor …'

'Ah, there you are again! Why didn't you get here earlier?'

'Forgive me please, I had …' But the baldy had disappeared again.

So, what had he done? He'd fought a battle, the same as on most other nights and, as always, he'd lost. But the world just shrugged its shoulders!

The pharmacist reappeared: 'Three marks fifty.'

'I don't have that much,' Tobias muttered.

'Well, alright,' the pharmacist said, 'I'll put it on the tab again, but you'd better pay. Understand?'

'Thank you very much,' Tobias whispered. 'Good evening'.

Now all his worries had vanished; there were no more thoughts, no more problems or questions as he clasped the eternal poison, folding his hands around the hexagonal bottle as though in prayer. He himself was life now, and his heart drowned out the world!

In the men's room at the café he shot up three times in a row, then carefully packed up the bottle and syringe and placed them back into the pocket of his trousers.

Now he felt free and light-hearted, as playful as a young god! He entered the café beaming with a smile for the young ladies and turning up his nose at the elegant gentlemen.[2] In the blink of an eye he'd fly up to the ceiling like Icarus, the divine youth, smiling and singing as he slid down from the canopy out front and circled on to the crackling stars.

II

Swinging over to the shiny marble table, he sat himself down between the chattering women and men. He ordered and lit one of the tangy cigarettes that were his companions in sorrow and joy.

But when he looked up through the aromatic smoke pouring from his mouth, *he could see the menacing night – that night, his night, shattering these short minutes of serene rush with its black fist,* advancing inexorably with a dark, agonising new intoxication, *the endlessly stretched out rhapsody of which would torture his ears from here on.*

What was it that distorted the faces across from him at the table, which had just been smiling? What did they mean, the squinting glances these people gave him and then tellingly and disapprovingly shared amongst each other?

See? They even crouched together now, and began to whisper …

He listened intently … and there you had it! Clearly, someone had spoken the word, the fatal word that towered over the firmament of his nights and slowly cut him into pieces, a remorseless machine even in its sound: *'Co-caine!* … *Co-caine!'* Bit by bit, it cut him up, until someday soon he would be pulverised entirely.

Little by little, panic filled pale Tobias' eyes. That man over there: he had unmistakably heard him say, incredibly quietly and yet clearly at the same time: 'That monster pumps himself full of cocaine every night!'

His heart was beating furiously. Something choked his clammy neck, a ghostly hand went through his shivering hair, and a cold sweat broke out on his backbone.

Get up! Away from here! *The big whip was already whizzing through the air over his head, banging and cracking loudly.* He paid with trembling hand, got up dizzily and, in a state of half paralysis, turned and fled, away from that cauldron.

Looking back as he stormed out, he noticed how the others had already become aware of him. They were laughing and pointing at Tobias.

A fat man, all red in the face, slapped himself on the thigh whilst roaring with laughter and then straightened up again, his red head ready to snap off and tumble down behind the chair. The horror! The revolving door spat Tobias out into the street.

But even there he couldn't find any peace.

People halted and stared at him. Harmless passers-by shook their heads and waited for Tobias to approach so they could take a closer look. He couldn't possibly stay here!

Keeping himself close to the houses, he hurried up Joachimsthaler Street in the direction of the station: a hunted animal startled by every shop-window that bathed him in light.

What did he have left in his misery, *now God screamed at him in scorn from the nocturnal clouds and the archangels were shaking their iron fists, making the streets resound with clattering noises?* What else remained but the sacred poison he carried in his pocket?

The tears welled up in his throat as he disappeared into the station hall to enter the public toilets once again; he, *the constant guest, the filthy woodlouse, the dung beetle.*

There, *just like the twitter of the sweet birds in the twilight,* the railway officials were blowing their whistles ... Suddenly, the turnstile of the ticket booth gave way, and the whole place turned to stare at him, this man who came staggering into the toilets like a drunk.

He locked himself up in one of the cubicles. What kind of life was this? The life of a corpse! Oh, despised and beloved poison, cocaine, cocaine (… the machine cut away – *click-clack, click-clack* – one more piece of him …).

Up above, a train came thundering into the station. … That must be the Riviera Express, Tobias mused … Yes, blue shores crowned by fluttering doves, pine- and orange groves and that blissful mountain, Santa Margherita … He took two more shots, one in each thigh.

This relieved him for a moment. … Riviera, he thought, Riviera, Santa Margherita …

Then he prayed, muttering: *'Please, dear God, you blessed Excellence, grant me that I perish silently with the next injection!'*

As he left the station toilets, the enormous vaulted space seemed to tremble with noise. The street clock warned him with a threatening straightened finger: midnight.

The entrance hall was roaring with traffic. The shrieks and cries of a devilish horde drilled into Tobias' ears as he forced himself through the – apparent – crowd, feeling naked and ashamed.

Didn't these people, this mocking and malicious mob, have anything else to do than ambush him, gathering at the station at midnight in order to enjoy the spectacle – how he, the cocaine addict, came crawling out of his sewer with his shirt sticking tightly to his bleeding arms and legs? Curse them! And curse his light-coloured attire … There, weren't those bloodstains?

He moistened his fingertips to rub out the spots.

Leaving the exit, he was about to plunge himself into the bustle of the road, but then suddenly took a turn and went to hide under the overpass.

III

There were two ladies on the corner opposite the station exit. Tobias gasped when he saw them: how on earth did they get here?

It was his mother and sister. But shouldn't they be in Cologne?

Obviously, they had to be in Cologne! But who really knew? Perhaps the stationmaster had called them to Berlin by telegraph, so they could witness their son and brother star in the same entertaining drama that the audience of Berlin West enjoyed each night; an amusing tragicomedy called 'The Sewer Prince' or 'My God, why hast Thou forsaken me' – a spectacle a lot more interesting and less expensive than what you found at the Palace Theatre or Nelson's playhouse.

They were standing on the corner in the brutal bluish glow of the arc lamp, their clothes fluttering about their bodies. There was a sound, as if their bones were rattling. *Or could it be his?* His knees were shaking, and so were his hands. *How thin they were!* Peering through his spread fingers, the many lamps became like confused, flittering cold moons, jumping off their black posts with a slight puff and then shattering on the asphalt.

The two female figures stood there motionless. Right, he knew that trick. They were acting cool but keeping a sharp eye on him all the while!

... My little blonde sister, dear Dotz, why won't you let me be? And you, Miss Sch..., Eveline or Ernestine – however your surname is pronounced; you, dear mother, why? On my back again? And so far from home! From the borders of Germany all the way to Berlin, only to frighten your *lost son*? Worthy, thrice worthy your mother love! ... What are you standing there? How can this be? Those faces!

A wave raced through his heated brain, and he mustered up his courage. Anger seized him. He stepped in the direction of the two figures, intending to pass the underground station where its stairs, adorned with stylised lamps, spewed out onto the road.

But a black crowd of people began to well up from the throat of the underground system and quickly began to surround him. Once again, his ears were tortured by shrieks. Breathing rapidly, he managed to escape this new danger and rushed off to the corner where the two ladies were standing.

Standing? Standing?

All he could see were two advertising signs, in black and gold, glaring at him outrageously. No women there, not a single person! ... Only a miserable dog that slowly dragged itself around the corner, sniffed a little and then did its usual business.

Tobias could feel his lungs becoming heavy, black and velvety. He crept into a doorway, quickly bared his forearm and injected a new dose of cocaine, half-dead for fear of being spotted.

IV

There you had it! Just for a moment the twinkling stars stood still again. Holy, holy poison! Tobias could feel and see the demon looming in the night sky, and it was as familiar to him as it was awe inspiring. He understood and whispered at the heavens: *'You are Death, Grace and Life. There is no God beside you!'*

He stepped back into the street.

At the intersection of Kurfürstendamm he entered the green-lit public toilets. An elderly man was putting his clothes in order as Tobias went over to a cubicle and prepared to urinate.

Tobias felt watched and helplessly flitted his hands over his suit. He couldn't hold still for a second. He turned around and stepped into a different cubicle, rummaging through every pocket in his suit in search of the bottle and syringe, until at last he looked up helplessly into the eyes of the man, who was about to leave and who scrutinised him coldly.

When he finally took off, Tobias stayed behind in utter despair … For God's sake! He must have been a detective, a medical officer, or even a representative of his mother, whom he'd run into earlier and who was hiding from him now!

For minutes, Tobias stood there helplessly in that reeking octagonal room, where slimy water drooled down the walls and at intervals produced sudden spluttering noises as if it wanted to spit on him.

He was convinced they were standing outside, encircling the restroom, forming a silent cordon. Handcuffs rattling, a straitjacket ready to be wrapped around him. A lump stuck in his throat; it stung with drought. The thirst! The thirst! … At his wit's end and prepared for the worst, he eventually left the booth and staggered out into the open.

He was perplexed to find no one lying in wait for him.

But there (his eyes popped out with the sudden fright…), there stood the old man and he whistled … he whistled loudly, once, twice!

Stop! Stop! Tobias ran towards him. He shivered as he took off his hat and addressed the man breathlessly: 'Don't be alarmed, sir, about my excitation! I've had a terrible experience! I assure you, really. Believe me, *I'm not mad! Not yet!* And I'm not drunk or intoxicated either! Believe me! Do not whistle for your people! Let me go!'

Startled, the man examined him from head to toe. He took a step back and said: 'What do you mean? I don't understand. What have I got to do with you? I'm whistling at my dogs.'

He whistled again. A dark-coloured shepherd came running and jumped up at its master with a wagging tail.

'Forgive me', Tobias murmured, and he quickly withdrew. This surely was a set-up! He'd noticed the secretive glance in that man's eyes, alright! It was time to find somewhere safe.

Tobias went in the direction of the Kaiserallee and ran below the trees for a while until his lungs were about to burst.[3] He stopped and looked around. It was late at night and there was no one to be seen. The street clock told half past twelve.

V

Here, in the shadow of the bushes, he took off his jacket, put it down on the pavement against the trunk of a tree and rolled up his shirt sleeves, exposing large dark spots that gave off the peculiar smell of spilled blood. With gnashing teeth he took two more injections, slowly and with utmost precision.

He held up the bottle against the distant lamplight. It was still two-thirds full. Reassured, he shoved it back into his trousers pocket, pulled out the other bottle and cleansed his upper arm with ether. He did the same with his forehead and neck.

The bushes in the front gardens were whispering, and one of the last trams approached from the distance.

Quickly, Tobias put his clothes in order.

Oh, how he wished he could be at home right now, to stomach the misery behind locks and bolts. But he knew he couldn't go to his furnished room. The landlady would have locked his door and hid the key to prevent him from getting in.

Where could he turn in his need? Bareheaded, he stood under the starry skies. Should he just wander around all night, as he'd done so often, only to end up being met by the grey morning alongside the Spree canal, or near the gasworks as it rose through the fog like a fist?

The ether had somehow diminished the spell of frenzied excitement he was under, although he could feel his pulse was still flying, rising, racing. Or was it the solitude, the absence of other people that gave him this relative calm?

He began to march, with the drug addict's toxic tenacity that cancelled all feeling in his muscles and tendons, down the long Kaiserallee to the Wilmersdorf-Friedenau station.[4] There, he veered off and soon found himself in front of a large apartment building.

This was where Marion, his saintly friend from the café, lived in a large studio.

The front door was locked. He whistled a couple of times and called out: 'Marion, Marion!'

It was in vain. She was sure to be asleep.

As he waited, pacing to and fro, the night air from the wastelands on the outskirts of the city blew around him and he could feel the black skies weighing down on him once more. The stars were heavy with viscous drops. The tall buildings oppressed him. The wind sang in the swaying arc lamps as they scattered their mad and dazzling light.

Fear took hold of him again. He looked about him anxiously and then ducked into a dark corner where he administered two new shots.

Ha! Straightaway that fever, that yellow flame lit up in him again! His brow crackled, his eyes widened and fixed in a stare as he shifted restlessly from one foot to the other.

He had almost forgotten what he wanted, as footsteps approached the house.

A gentleman halted at the front door, rattling his keys.

Tobias went up to the man and greeted him shyly.

'No one is answering,' he stuttered. 'I'm here to escort a lady to her sick relative.'

The man let him in silently and relocked the door.

Tobias switched on the light and hurried up the stairs.

Suddenly it occurred to him it might be better to let the

man enter his apartment first. He halted. As soon as the man reached the first floor, he opened the door and stepped inside his home. The door closed and the light, on a timer, went out. Through the colourful windows of the stairwell, the trembling light of the streetlamps formed fantastical patterns.

Tobias nervously sneaked up to the fourth floor, dreading each landing with mortal fear.

Upstairs, on the fourth floor, a door that stood ajar brought him into a little corridor with a skylight. At its end was a heavy iron door, which led to Marion's studio.

Tobias switched the light on again. He placed the bottle and the pouch with his syringes down. Then he rubbed his bloody arms once more with ether and took another injection.

Powerful new hallucinations began.

He turned around. Voices rose from the bottom of the staircase on the ground floor; the voices of several people about to come up. Confused, semi-audible whispering. He managed to make out a few phrases: *'This really has to stop … It's a scandal … That pig is ruining himself and his family … To the asylum with him! … We'll drag him into the car … You grab him right away! … And make sure he doesn't drink that bottle, it would do the chap in!'*

Tobias shivered. He was dripping with sweat (… or was it blood?). He could hear the voice of his mother as the light went out again: *Tobias, my son! Tobias, I beg you! … Tobias, Tobias! … Tobias … '*

The voice was a plaintive. *Clack, clack, clack!* They were mounting the stairs, steadily coming closer. All the while the whispering continued.

Did he have the nerve to switch the light back on? …
He did.

… There, before him, at his feet, still wriggling ever so
slightly, lay the body of his dying mother. And next to her,
dressed in black, her face shrouded in black veils, his sister
squatted down, crying softly with a sunken head.

Tobias shrank back and turned away, pressing his hot face
against the wall.

VI

His heart was pounding like a hammer in his skull. After a
while he turned around again. The ghost had disappeared. He
quickly gave himself a new fix and then started knocking on
the door, quiet at first, but then more and more loudly.

He bent down to the keyhole and with muted voice called
'Marion! Marion!', constantly looking over his shoulder to
make sure no one crept up on him from behind.

At last he could see the light come on. A shadow moved
across the floor and approached the door. A thin, sleepy
voice, Marion's voice, anxiously asked: 'Who's there, for
God's sake'?

'It's me, Tobias … Marion, open up, I have to get in.'

The door was opened, softly screeching on its hinges.
Tobias staggered inside, his body shuddering with wild
spasms from the series of shots he had taken in such rapid
succession.

Marion stood before him in her nightgown, a candle in her
hand. She knew Tobias and was aware of his condition; this
wasn't the first time he'd come to call on her at night.

She was tired – it must have been half past two – but she didn't betray her annoyance. Without a word, she prepared a camp bed for him that stood behind a partition.

'Lie down,' she said, 'and give me the cocaine.'

She knew she was asking in vain; that he wouldn't surrender the cocaine even if she tried to force him to.

Tobias shook his head. He had put the candle on a chair and sat perched on the edge of the camp bed, staring at his friend as she laid back down.

'Did you close the door properly? Are the windows shut?' he asked her.

'Yes, of course!'

He took off his jacket.

Marion moaned and looked away.

He was a ghastly sight indeed!

Both of his sleeves were stiff and darkened with blood down to the wrists. They gave off a foul smell.

'Please, hurry,' Marion whispered, 'and don't stain the sheets with blood.'

Still turned away from him, she was overcome with nausea. Suddenly she got up and vomited in the corner of the room, crying to herself.

Desperate and distraught, Tobias began to howl. He shook his fists above his head and gazed up at the ceiling with his eyes open wide.

Marion, as pale as a sheet, rushed towards him and put her hand over his mouth.

'Quiet, quiet,' she whispered into his ear, 'no one must hear you, or they'll kick me out of here!'

No! No one could hear these desperate people, *least of all that merciful father, whose unforgiving black figure appeared in front of the large studio windows; rigid, unmoved and immobile!*

'Come on, lie down and be quiet,' Marion said, 'I want to sleep. Put out the light.'

Tobias took all his clothes off and Marion looked away in fright. Even the lower edge of his shirt was covered in blood from the injection wounds to his thighs. It was his only shirt and he had been wearing it for three weeks: his landlady in Charlottenburg was holding back all the other laundry as collateral for the rent he owed. He reeked and was disgusting to himself, revolting, loathsome.

He placed the medicine bottle on the chair and put away the syringe, stretched out on the camp bed without covering himself, and blew out the candle.

Breathless, he waited a couple of minutes. He lay still and stared at the ceiling which, on his side of the room, was half window, the same window that also covered the upper half of the walls.

Marion didn't stir. Night crept through the room, slow and slimily. Dark sticky threads seemed to cross the studio, back and forth from one wall to the other, emitting the smell of clotted blood mixed with the cloyed perfume of cocaine and the more astringent tone of ether.

It was deathly quiet. Marion appeared to be asleep. Only the nocturnal wind regularly rattled the window panes. Tobias was grinding his teeth loudly, the way he always did when the cocaine poisoning had reached a certain stage. It distorted his face, and his temples rippled like waves. Didn't some limping old lady on Alexanderplatz just recently flee from him in terror on seeing his contorted expression?

His thinking stopped. He just lay there motionless, staring at the glass ceiling. From time to time he injected a shot of cocaine in the dark, no longer taking even the slightest bit of care. He could feel the blood running over his battered thighs and his ragged upper and lower arms. It undoubtedly dripped into the sheets Marion had begged him to keep clean as well, but he couldn't give a damn anymore. He was already poisoned to such a degree that he had to keep fixing up at increasingly shorter intervals, *like something as self-evident as breathing or eating, simply to stay alive at all.*

Suddenly he became aware of shadows gliding over the glass walls and roof of the studio. He observed them suspiciously for a while.

When he looked closely, he became convinced they were the shadows of people – heads, arms, legs – who were up to something on the edge of the roof. Now a faint whispering even crept through the glass. Tobias could distinguish three voices; male voices, talking eagerly. He followed the shadows warily. He could see them handing each other tools – levers, pliers, crowbars – and the faint exclamations fit their movements exactly.

'*Look out,*' he heard. '*One … two … three … Go!*' Then a distinct cracking.

A draft entered the room, a cold breeze apparently coming from above. He could feel it over his entire body.

A rapidly intensifying panic took hold of him. They were burglars! Or detectives! … Didn't the painter Ludwig M.,[5] from Südwestkorso district, not far from here, tell him about a burglar he had met in the storage room outside his studio?

His throat burnt with a paralysing fear. He lay there helplessly, bleeding, sick to death. Marion was asleep, a defenceless girl. If those were burglars, they'd deal with the two of them in no time. And if they were detectives, they'd both be taken into protective custody, and charges would be pressed against him, Tobias. He would be sent to an institution for years, and he wouldn't get any cocaine.

He got up quietly and shook his friend awake.

She had been sleeping soundly and rose with a start.

'What is it? What's wrong?'

Tobias pointed up to the glass ceiling and whispered: 'Do you see? Do you see those people there?'

The shadows were still moving.

'What people?' Marion asked fearfully.

'There, there; the shadows on the roof,' said Tobias, 'that's burglars or secret agents. For Christ's sake, Marion, what should we do?'

Marion, now fully awake, gave him a horrified look.

'Nonsense,' she said. 'That's the shadow of the arc lamps below in the street.'

Tobias shook his head.

'Arc lamps don't cast any shadows,' he whispered, staring up at the ceiling with a twisted expression.

Marion began to doubt his sanity. *Is he really already so far gone?* she thought.

A vague fear crept up her spine. To be at the mercy of this madman, alone in a building asleep! She didn't know what to do. If she could just calm him down, then they'd take it from there when the day came. 'But surely those are the shadows of the trees down below and the chimneys and eaves on the roof,' she told him. 'The arc lamp is swaying in the wind down there; that's why the shadows are moving. Go to bed, lie down!'

This did not put Tobias entirely at ease, but it calmed him a little. He would stay awake and alert.

'Where do you have your revolver? You've got a small revolver, haven't you; where is it?' he asked.

But she made sure he wouldn't get his hands on the gun.

'I don't know where it is right now,' she said. 'Just lie down, there are no burglars.'

Tobias decided to search for the revolver as soon as Marion fell asleep. He lay back and spied on the shadows that swayed back and forth unceasingly, appearing to reach out for all manner of things.

A dim light already fell through the glass panes, their edges becoming clearer and sharper. The first streaks of dawn were breaking through.

VII

Tobias was horrified when he held the bottle up against the light. Only a tiny amount of the fluid remained, hardly a finger's width from the bottom. An unnameable dread gripped his throat … No more cocaine!

And then the day broke, *that hated day*, which would force him to go out and face the people, *who were all his enemies and of whom he was petrified.* He tossed and turned on the bed in dull despair. His head grew hotter and hotter from the fear, until a burning rage drove him to take two more injections. Then he drank the last remaining liquid from the bottle. The interior of his mouth felt numb and hairy, like velvet. He ran his finger deep inside, as far as his throat.

The great yearning had returned! What should he do now? What good was the day or living to him without the poison which his body, his soul, his entire being craved?

Gone was the fear of burglars and detectives, vanished the terror of the madhouse! Only one feeling burnt within him – the inflexible, inexorable, irresistible, the philosophically foundationless drive, the longing for the poison that was life itself, the air he breathed, being and time to him!

He lit the candle with feverish hands. He wanted to make absolutely sure there really was nothing left in the bottle. True, he'd just emptied it into his mouth that very second, but his mad cravings overpowered his sense of logic. *It could be, couldn't it,* that there was still a tiny bit left in there? Or perhaps he'd bought *two bottles* earlier that night without thinking of it until now? Or maybe there was still one from last time, hidden somewhere in the room?

He held the bottle against the candlelight. No, no, no! Nothing left! He turned it upside-down and stuck his tongue deep inside the bottleneck. There was nothing left!

A distant thunderstorm seemed to enclose the room, and the windows were lit up by a reddish shimmer. The rumble of mighty daybreak struck him dumb.

He got up from the bed and searched the room, crawling on his knees and smearing himself with the thick drops of blood that lay scattered across the floor. He didn't trust his eyesight and took every object in his hands, touching it and holding it close to his face. Could this be a bottle of cocaine, or perhaps that? Weren't his eyes deceiving him? *Was that which looked like a slipper, really a slipper and not something else? Who could really tell?*

But however much he searched, he didn't find a thing.

Creeping on his stomach, he rummaged through the lowest compartment of the dresser and stumbled upon the gun and a supply of cartridges. He placed them both on a chair. But the shadows were gone.

The windows were aglow with a pleasant soft pink light from which a new summer's day emerged, clear, calm and majestic in measure. *Hear, the sweet birds were whistling again, chirping at the light.*

VIII

Tobias got up and turned towards the window.

He stood there speechless as the overwhelming light that broke in the east was poured out over him, this wasted, bloodily mangled body, unconsciously surrounding him like a heavenly bath. Tobias opened the window and shivered when the cool breeze hit him.

Marion, that holy angel, was fast asleep. Tobias went to the bathroom next door and filled up the tub with warm water. He washed his wounds and his entire body; every now and then it twitched nervously at the touch of his hands. Then he wrapped himself in his bloody shirt and got dressed. The small alarm clock showed almost seven.

He went to Marion's bed and observed the sleeping woman for a long while. Eventually, he bent down and kissed her on the forehead.

She awoke.

'Marion,' he said, 'I must go. Do you have any bread here? I'm hungry.'

'Hold on,' she answered, 'I'll get up and cook you something.'

He stepped back behind the screen and sat down on his bed. Large blood stains covered the pillows and sheets that lay all crumpled across the bed and on the floor. On the chair next to the bed Tobias found the revolver. He loaded the six chambers of the cylinder and took the gun with him.

He had calmed down entirely and felt inconceivably tired. Marion had dressed and gone to the kitchen in order to prepare the soup on the stove.

Tobias silently stared out into the fallow fields of the suburbs.

They were still building here. There were parcels of land, fenced in with wire mesh and overgrown with ragged grass, and paved roads with no houses as yet that crossed each other and peacefully ran towards the glow of the morning sun. *The birds were singing gently.* The sky was of a deep azure through which fleecy clouds were slowly moved along by a gentle breeze.

Marion brought in the soup; it was thick and nutritious and it tasted good. She gave him some slices of dry bread which he ate with it. As always, after the stomach numbing effect of the poison had waned, it gave way to a powerful hunger and thirst. He finished two plates of the soup. Marion was friendly and chatted with him good-humouredly. She didn't ask him to give up cocaine; she knew it would be useless.

He was deeply grateful to this gentle creature, the only one who didn't turn her back on him, the pariah without friends who was spat out by every house like some revolting leper.

'Do you have any money?' she asked him.

He shook his head silently.

'I have one mark left, of which I can give you fifty pfennigs. And here's some food stamps for the soup kitchen.'

She handed them over.

Tobias laid his head on the edge of the table and began to cry, bursting out in deep sobs. He took the good girl's hand and buried his mad face in it, covering it in tears. Marion softly stroked his hair: *'Poor Tobias!'*

IX

He remained seated for a while. Then he grabbed his hat, kissed her hand and took off.

In the stairwell he made sure no one could see him. It was strange to descend here, where the ghosts had frightened him out of his wits. There was a stale taste in his mouth.

Downstairs, outside the front door, he was greeted by the radiant sunlight.

Tobias walked out into the open, aimlessly wandering the empty streets. There was hardly anyone out at this early hour.

Suddenly, the bells of the surrounding churches began to toll, creating one continual chant that reverberated through the air in a manner more delicate and more ethereal than he'd ever heard before.

He strolled over beautifully laid out squares and admired the colourful houses that rose up to the song-filled sky with incomprehensible serenity, looking as if they were polished. It was a Sunday. High up in the heavens small bright clouds sailed by and gathered in the harbour of the horizon.

Tobias arrived at the Kaiserallee.

The approaching trams raced past him with ringing bells in a swirl of life and movement.

At the Friedrich-Wilhelm-Platz he wandered around the red church.[6] He wanted to go in. But as he approached the entrance, he could sense the presence of people.

Once again that dark dread took hold of him, that anxiety born of night and despair, which drove him away from all company, all humanity and all society.

He had nowhere left to go!

He stopped and opened his hand. He stared at it a long while, as if in deep thought. Then he looked at his greasy suit and his decrepit boots. Bloodstains seeped through the sleeves of his light jacket, and there were stains on his trousers as well.

He hunched up when he heard footsteps behind him.

It was the priest on his way to church.

Tobias carried on slowly, shuffling alongside the front gardens of the avenue.

Fathers, mothers and children were sitting out having their breakfast on the little balconies. *Merry laughter resounded,* and Tobias stared up furtively. He felt hungry again.

… *Then he realised he would not live to see the evening of that Sunday.*

No longer would that mighty demon take hold of him and cast him into darkness.

He had nothing to look forward to. He was sick and forsaken, an outcast with no possessions. No food, no money, no clothes, no home, no friends or fellow men. And he lacked the will, the strength to acquire any of these things.

The poison, which was his only destiny, loomed over the city like a giant animal, hovering over the horizon and over his existence; *the inescapable Charybdis waiting to suck him up.*

Living like a reject, he'd waste away his entire life, from morning to evening, until one night he'd finally go mad.

He stepped into a doorway and took out the revolver. He cocked it and contemplated the best angle. Eventually, he opened his mouth and pressed the barrel of the weapon up against his palate. *It was alright like this.*

He pulled the trigger. The shot rang out, echoing through the building.

Tobias collapsed into a kneeling position.

Residents rushed to the scene and found him dead. Pieces of his brain were splattered everywhere; on the walls, on the railings and on the steps of the stairway.

Outside the birds were singing and a tram clamoured through the morning, down the avenue, on its way into Berlin.

Originally published as *Kokain: Novelle, mit sieben Zeichnungen von Felixmüller* (Dresden: Dresdner Verlag von 1917, 1918).

NOTES

1. i.e. Kantstrasse.

2. The café in question, the Romanisches Café, was heavily damaged during World War II. In 1965, the Europa Center was erected in its place.

3. Kaiserallee was renamed Bundesallee in 1950.

4. The Wilmersdorf-Friedenau station no longer exists; it was replaced by the present-day Bundesallee station.

5. The painter meant is Ludwig Meidner.

6. i.e. the Zum guten Hirten church.

THE HUMBLING –
A DANCE OF DEATH

I

Who is more called to feel the powers over themselves than the poet? Who is more called to drink up all gruesomeness of their echoing grottoes than he, the chosen *kat exochen*, the affirmer, the eternal fighter on the Mount of Olives, who says: 'if it be possible, let this cup pass from me, for I will drink it; not as I will but as thou wilt! …' He lives on all islands; he falls in every city; frozen sparrow, floats down to every park; and every night is hostile to him! – Only those who serve may command! … So he, the prince, serves and becomes king over night and darkness, triumphant caller and ruler of light. – And he fell into the (wretched) wasteland of oriental poison: he, the one called, Tobias Sternraffer, the poet. –

One o'clock passed! … Full of terror he stepped across the floating bridge. The pontoons groaned, squelchy water animals under his hurried gait. The cathedral, a startled giant hare, fled into the murky distance with long ears. A lost steamer hastened in the darkness with splashing wheels. The bleeding light of a factory on the shore pulsed through the skeleton of rods and greasy window eyes. His hand in the doctor's bag encircled the medical bottle. A deep dread in the front of his brain, on the periphery of the skull, in the eyes, in his neck. And a macabre urge, an unfathomable, inscrutable, irresistible yearning for the poison in his spine: – so he sat in the tram, hidden. He could not wait to arrive home.

His mother and sister were already asleep, but the cat glowed in his room. He lit the gas and laid out upon the chair the bottle, syringe, absorbent cotton, cloth and candle. He had hardly removed his great coat when he gave himself two strong injections (Sol. Hydro. Cocaine 0.06) in the upper arm. His feet elevated from the floor, the hair steamed, he floated on the ceiling and drank in the glow of the gas light. He undressed most eagerly.

He still was not in bed, but already felt the dark fabric floating down upon him, almost wrapping around him tightly, thickly enveloping mouth, nose, ears and lungs and pressing him into a corner. There he contracted till he was very small. His eyes opened wide; the pupils expanded into two immeasurable black shafts … Ah!, the pressure fled from his body! – Hastily he took two further shots. He immediately felt better and infinitely calm. His eyes closed. But they once again opened like two dark moons: wide! wide! … His hand shook slightly. He fled to bed. – The furniture began to whisper and the window curtains produced soft music. The room rocked, a slowly sinking ship. Stop! They could watch him! … He carefully veiled the windows, locked the door and hung his hat on the handle. – But the photographs on the dresser could be secretly used as mirrors by the observers! He laid them flat, grabbed a mirror himself and furtively watched the proceedings in the part of the room he was forced to turn his back to.

The fear increased … the wall paper grew animated with eyes that slowly circled up and around, gazing sternly. He started and looked around. But he immediately threw his body back because there was something moving under the sofa … could it be his sister, who gave his sleeping mother light signals regarding his state and the number of injections? … He jumped up, looked under the sofa, took a new shot, laughed (it was the cat), extinguished the gas light and once again laid down in his bed.

He lay there bug-eyed. The cat crept quietly around the room. – He was gripped by a new fear. He heard voices clearly, the voices of his mother and his sister. He quickly took a shot. Now they were a little silent. Yet suddenly the doorbell rang (in the middle of the night!), the door opened, someone stepped into the next room. Tobias could now somehow (he did not further contemplate why) see into the next room with his hand mirror. – There a light was on. His mother and sister, wearing nightgowns, sat at the table. The man who had entered was Dr Pagenstecher, the pharmacist from whom he obtained the cocaine. He had his hat in his hand, wore an overcoat and shook his head slowly and compassionately. His mother cried. Now Tobias clearly heard his sister speak: 'Isn't it terrible with Tobias? … How his eyes open wide! A doctor should be called! He'll go crazy!' The pharmacist nodded sadly. His mother sobbed: 'Yes, Mr Pagenstecher, fetch the doctor!' The pharmacist turned and left. His mother had buried her head in her hands on the table in deep sorrow.

II

Oh, God! The doctor! ... – Tobias jolted up and tried to light the candle with feverish hands. Only the sixth match caught fire. He took a shot. In the meantime the daylight broke through the veiled window, slowly and grey, creeping. Tripping over the cat that sat upright, holding the little mirror in its front paws, Tobias opened the door to his room, at first quietly and then with force, and stared piercingly into the corridor. In the background there stood an old chest and sitting upon it Tobias clearly saw the form of his mother, who sought to hide her countenance riven by grief. His sister Ly had hidden behind the clothes on the coat stand and clucked disapprovingly with her tongue. Tobias stared for a long time in that direction. Finally he stuttered into the hallway (and his voice stuck on his gums limply and in tatters): Mother! ... Don't bother! ... I can see you! ... I only took a single shot!' The blood rose coldly into his head with this lie, but at the moment he considered it necessary in order to calm his mother, who had large tears pouring out of her eyes. She did not move. 'Well, I ... I ... I can see it! ...' Tobias said. As he turned away he saw his sister dart into the room, how she disappeared just behind the drapes at the window. He re-locked the door.

He hesitantly crept towards the drapes, but before he had reached them Ly had jumped through the closed window. He went and checked to see if she was maybe still hanging onto the window sill. But she lay below, smashed on the street, moving her anguished body.

People slowly gathered. – All of Tobias' extremities trembled. He sat down on his bed and gave himself two consecutive shots. With the second he had pushed the needle in too deep. A thin, light-red rivulet quickly welled up, crept from his upper arm to his wrist, dripped onto his thigh and coursed down his leg to the sole of his foot. It looked like a railroad line on a map. The cotton absorbed itself red, regardless of how often Tobias tried to stanch the blood. Jeering flow! Finally it seemed to him as if he was bleeding from a thousand pricks and from all bodily openings. He was seized by mortal fear. He let the streams follow their course. Now it became broad daylight. A crystalline sun sent blinding cold rays on the surrounding high five-story buildings. The huge roofs seemed to flatten and the sunrays fell upon the street like millions of needles. Tobias dragged himself to the window to look for his sister. – On the street it was blackened by people, a pushing, thronging crowd that silently and persistently looked up at Tobias, with faces full of anger and *schadenfreude*.

Tobias frantically searched around on the floor. But what was he looking for? … Needles, his sister, or a part of her graceful, shattered little body? His hands and knees were completely dirty because his exhausted mother had long stopped cleaning Tobias' room. Countless matchboxes, cotton, drops of wax and blood lay around. Tobias gathered all of it in his hands, fiddled with it and examined it precisely. He was afraid that all of these objects could be his sister, and that he just saw so poorly … once again he came close to the window. Down below the throng backed up, looking up attentively, and people questioned each other, murmuring. But even the roofs of the building across the street, all the windows and all the balconies were teeming with people, men and women, in part even with telescopes and opera glasses, but all of them assembled purely because of him and looking at him. His mother and sister, freezing in nightdresses, were among them. Iris, the cat, strolled sardonically over the thousands of heads with ironic paws. Dr Pagenstecher, the pharmacist, stood on the middle balcony and explained Tobias Sternraffer's horrible case, gesticulating to a bevy of police with his arms. They listened. Helmets and truncheons nodded. Although Tobias did not understand a word, it was unquestionable that they were speaking about him, about him!

Then all the police officers suddenly turned around and peered intently at Tobias. One advanced (the crowd rushed, a sea) and yelled over at him (it was the police captain in a glittering uniform):

'Hey! Sir! You there! For heaven's sakes! Stop that now! Aren't you ashamed of yourself!? You animal!!' Applause, hand clapping among the people below. Newcomers continued to arrive from adjoining streets, the balconies became more and more filled and a tumultuous, echoing racket arose: 'Hey! You there! Hey! Mr Sternraffer! Mr Sternraffer! ... Stop! Stop! Knock it off! Hey! Mr Sternraffer!'

Several of them jumped down from the balconies and hurriedly climbed up the façade of the building towards Tobias' bedroom window. He babbled, drenched in sweat:

'Now ... now ... But ... but ... the building ... will break ...'

Indeed it did break. – At first the tall wardrobe rocked, grinning satanically. The bed doubled over. A tumult arose, a droning! Violet suns danced. The wardrobe and furniture slowly bent far over! Tobias tried to scream; the sound remained stuck in his throat. While falling he saw how all of the balconies crumbled and whistled into the depths along with the observers ... everything sank in the ocean of racket and light ...

III – REQUIEM

But the pharmacist (... don't you see? ...) is JESUS CHRIST, who sits above the collapsed buildings and over the fallen people and shakes his head with compassion. He has his hat in his hand and will call the doctor. He pulls a large jaw harp from his medical bag. He cries and as the tears fall on the reed it quietly sounds: you son of man! The heavens do not give a glance and a good word to the deathly dance of misery. A martyr's rain, muffled tears, crowns (oh, bitterness!) your heads. You poor skeletons! Swallowed by destitution and death, God ignites the shrine of the arduous brain ... You, oh man, are great! And you bear a crown of thorns, and crucifixion a thousand fold! ...

... And Tobias Sternraffer, who sees him, Tobias, lamented body in his mother's lap, yells! yells!:

Be good! Be good!!

Originally published as 'Die Erniedrigung – ein Totentanz', in *Die Aktion*, year 8, Vol. 1/2, pp. 19-24 (Berlin, 1918).

THREE FRAGMENTS FROM A WAR NOVELLA

I

Their heads, crazy orbs, were seething that evening in the village tavern. The rain whipped against the thin window panes. This often sounded like the distant pitter-patter of a great cavalry riding continuously through the village, charging forward with individual groups and retreating with others. The scent of rain permeated the wooden walls and saturated the billows of cigarette haze and tobacco that wandered over the confused faces. Two dim lamps swelled and rotated slowly on the ceiling, which seemed close by one moment, distant the next. A slow rhythm animated the limbs of the soldiers who lay around like mannequins, gone dead, on the tables and benches, shuffled slowly over the floor. In the corner a bad piano, a fake violin whose notes twanged with snappy beats through the room like strings. The fiddler's goggling eyes gleamed over the violin; he grinned diabolically when he saw how the notes moved the tightly packed throng like masks. Heads and shoulders swayed back and forth, staggering. One did not recognise the other. 'Comrade', 'beer', 'give me a light', 'the Russians', 'shot in the stomach', it screamed. Billiard balls banged. One soldier had a disagreement, was furious; his blood-red face looked as if split; the blow of an axe ran up to his drawn upper lip. Olaf cowered tightly in the corner. Something rotten decayed inside of him, a pale flame swelled on the inside. A waltz staggered from the music corner. ('*Les baisers sont flétris*', it sings along in Olaf.) An acrobat danced on his hands. Berlin, the great, glowing spider, was far away. It rolled off into the distance, tumbled over and pulled all of the cities in its web behind it. The wind stormed around the house; the music, the conversation creaked. All faces were blank, puffed up like dough. *People knew: outside the millions swarm.* The great serpent coils incessantly in the east and west. It circles around itself, spewing poison. A high forest of cannons stares into the clouds. Wide rivers of blood flow into the sea; islands of corpses decompose. But here new masses of flesh cower. White and cold is the tobacco smoke. Exhaustion sets in. They are silent for two, three seconds in which the images of beloved women seep sweetly and quietly from their inward gazing eyes. Then once again a din. Erid's countenance trembled large and clearly on the ceiling. A vein of vapour formed the movement of her shoulders. Olaf sank. People crawled into moist straw. Individual stars appeared, then rain again. Wet mice over hot lips. A distant trumpeter, slow signal. They stared into the darkness. Finally fell asleep, in the greying dawn, shivering.

II

A crashing vault, the night closes its black ring around the army. Fiery ribbons loop over the parted hair of those cowering. Tie the breath of the thousands tighter. Large sheaves of hay and the stench of cadavers roam through the passageways. Hidden little fires smoulder breathlessly and frightened, circled by shadowy gaunt countenances. Coarsely slurred orders creep further along the earthen walls of the trenches. They whisper, keep silent. But the sky rages; clods rise up within it; it crumbles, breaks. Do not huge black bowls fall from the sky, with frightened, small stars swimming in them? The field in front of the trenches is a seething hot lake. Waves of earth boil, hill-bubbles burst. It undulates. The grenades rise like geysers. They appear to come from the belly of the earth. Suddenly they hit in even beats. *Danse macabre!* Shrapnel sprays apart; all eyes stare up. Why suddenly the vision of memory: fireworks in the *Werkbund Exhibition* in Cologne on the river Rhine. Fire gushing from the Rhine bridge. Glistening terraces, fountains, flowery women, gold and the iridescent, sensually breath-taking beats of the *Tango Argentino?* Ah! Clouds darting across the nocturnal firmament? Escaping to the sea? The night roars. It bursts. The night is a clanging metal lid that has moved across the horizon. Now it splitters, and behind it the sun exults in raving fire. Sunken faces, cowering, bent over the gunstocks, garishly spit upon by fire, expressionless, masklike. The blood flickers through the bodies. Within one second three times through the eyes, heart, legs, brains; it knocks. *It wants out.* There, a crazy voice, cracking through the thicket of this silence. *'Storm! March – march!'* They flare up from the trenches, these buried flaming faces; the limbs jerk up. The arms churn like machine pistons. Suddenly Olaf feels the entire mechanism of his body. His muscles become taut, the eyes palpable in their sockets; he feels his hair growing, feels the play of sinews in his arms, legs, hands. The weapon is in his hand. Forward. The predators jump. They roar. Saliva flows from his mouth, snot from his nose, water from his eyes, pores, penis. And his brain lies on a plate, indeed, on a glass plate that turns at breakneck speed. It spurts out, to the north, south, forwards, backwards. Centrifugal force. The body rages. Yes: blood as well, blood also has to spray! And: to the left lies the North Sea, Baltic Sea, White Sea; the Black Sea to the right. They rise, the seas, high as a house. They crash into the land. They stalk around on long typhoon legs. And the sky encroaches. It vibrates with giant dark suns of black marble. And the forests sway. The stars dangle in their branches. And there is the enemy, the Russians. *Ah! Moscow, bells, snow!* 'Dogs! Friends! People! Animals! *We murderers! You Murderers!* Moscow! Berlin!' – 'Prusski stoi!' – 'Stoi, stoi' – 'Hurrah, urra!' – 'Hey!' – 'Halt!' – 'Ace!' Bayoneted in the paunch. Olaf thrusts, runs down, thrusts, shoots with his revolver. A blow to his shoulder. A grenade tears through a group of comrades. One of them falls into his arms, the neck-stump gurgles hot blood into his face. Backbone and brain become icy, rigid. The racket sounds near and far. Ah! The sea becomes smooth! He sinks into it.

III

A thousand flags storm in his soul. The *Tricolore* flames up out of his eyes. 'Ah! Midinette, I will ride you down!' Darting on the stairway, glittering dustily in the twilight, the ghosts of those green and blue nights, the intertwined hours of soul fusion. Ah! But the fronts arise in the East and West, cities gleaming from the sun clatter and a new day is stormed with trains by thousands whose steps drum through the midday streets of Berlin. Oh, shining fleet on the crystalline seas! Work rings out, rummages around. And the day lies open and reflects the hollowed out blue sky. He already stands in the room and she wafts him coolly, in a green veil; her hair once again lies unbearably smoothly, addictive, and the white in her eyes are bent moons above dreamy ponds. Let the dream continue! Shining capturing of the wild, naked, dancing day! And his new voice, blank and rising unshrouded: 'Do you love me, Erid?' – 'I love you, I was with you every day, I covered you with myself, Ole.' Yet he, hard: 'I love you, today. If you love me then abandon your husband, come with me. *I live in the cellar, where sun is a priceless Sunday. At night shoo the rats from my forehead. We will eat from one bowl, with one spoon, in turn. Come!*' She trembles. 'Ole!' – 'Come, my bride, my love, found through the eons!' – 'Are you serious, Ole? You know that I can't leave him. He …' And Olaf, interrupting: 'Yes. He makes your life easy. You can dream, sing, sleep. But there's one thing you can't do, poor woman: love. *A woman and you can't love!* Come! With me you can love. Help me hunger, work, fight. We will conquer life, and the deed will blossom, *the blessed deed …*' – She shrieks loudly: 'Ole! Are those your words? I can't love? And I love you, so deeply, so intimately, so supremely! Don't talk like that! Isn't that love, felt a thousand times, named a thousand times by you!' – 'No, Erid, not love. *Only its ghost!* Look how the cities buzz against the sky! *Work is, deeds are!* Not dreams. Vibrating exterior from glorious interior. Nothing creeping into itself (… ah, this *imitatio coitus* of the soul, he simultaneously thinks …). Roaring top from the silent depths. And blessed in-everything instead of above-everything. Poor! Come, *I will teach you about life and great love* (… little blond mooncalf, his heart laughs along

...). Completely mine, completely the world's, completely this day's. Hey, how purely the air moves, the mountains glow and the rivers flutter. And the cranes jangle. Pearl-like ships. And the sun buzzes, rejoicing disc! Come!' – 'I can't, I ... Ole ... are you Ole?' – 'I'm new. Come, we'll tie the knot. We'll travel to Paris, to London, to St. Petersburg, to Rome, to New York, the brotherly cities!' And she replies, singing: 'I don't know you anymore, Olaf, my love. Look, I sit in the arbour and the moon casts singing nets. And my soul is with you above the roofs of the great city. Your step a high cantilena, Olaf, my thou, my heart wandering outside. Behold, how the night effloresces from my eyes. Ah, they drain the sky, meeting you. And your last hand-kiss is a slow dance on this snow of your hand, Olaf. We fall asleep at the same time, our soul falls asleep. Where do our bodies lie, separated or close or far? We are intertwined, and the world is a pearl musical box in our breast, around which the nocturnal winds blow ...' She startles, her face exceedingly bright; it falls from the sky, a moonstone.

Originally published as 'Drei Fragmente aus einer Kriegsnovelle', in *Der Bunte Tag*, Dichtung der Jüngsten, Vol. 12/13 (Dresden: Dresdner Verlag von 1917, 1919).

THE DEATH OF THE DREAMER GAUTIER FÉMIN

(A FAREWELL AND A GREETING)

I

I don't want to claim that my friend Gautier Fémin, clerk in the house of Dreyfus & Co. in Paris, had always been a romantic dreamer. But during the time to which I am referring, his mistake was that he too easily and exclusively believed in 'Beauty': a concept, or (as he always corrected me) an experience with which he not in the least connected any kind of ethical or even practical goals. Thus an aesthete, as he frequently emphasised that beauty was purely there for its own sake, free of every tendency, removed from all realistic action, although it manifested itself in action (like a torso uncovered from rubble and dirt). – This was his second fallacy, and as he told me (in the hour of realization still entangled in confused mysticism) shortly before the event, the inner cause of his necessary death.

It is possible that his mistress, nameless at the time, in the hour of his complete rejection became the innocent bullet that executed his suicide. – Transplanted from Kristiania[1] to Paris for the sake of his study of music, Erid had met him in the salon of a young composer: – bringing him to his knees before the midnight sun landscape of her head and the cool otherness of her body. Not much later this woman was seen, under profligate ignorance of her husband as well as her previous friend, floating arm in arm with him through the colourful fields of the vespertine boulevards, lathering in the light cascades of the concert halls and theatre, growing hazy in the pink glow and perfume of the ateliers of befriended young painters. We often sat together occupied with other, burning conversations, or walked along the banks of the Seine in the evening, and he was missing, Gautier Fémin, the dreamer. Later I heard about him, that he coalesced more and more with Erid on such days, in sonorous silence or in light conversation (the words of which, however, golden and deep, silently fell inward as in a dripstone cave). Words and small actions passed between them from which a gaze suddenly blossomed, making him recognise the deepest essence of their unity. And on long walks, while they felt the forest edge, the ponds, and closer firmaments in Bois de Boulogne, sweet and new, flowing over them, he created a shared evangelical word for her, 'Thou-Being', within which they completed each other. Decimated creator of boundless idealism, transforming with all shocks of body and spirit under arched mutually internalised days, Gautier no longer recognised the spirit and purpose of the prosaic numbers of current accounts, the polyglot texts of oceanic business correspondence, the austere orders of the manager in the office of Dryfus & Co. After repeated incidences of poorly excused failing to appear to work, after the first mystical journey in the bed of his mistress

(… vessel for traveling through worlds in space endlessly filled with faces! …), crouching over the lectern, bleary and transfigured, in the evening of a singing end of May he found himself drifting past the houses of the Rue de la Banque towards the great boulevards, quietly appalled but yet quickly appeased: dismissed, his last wages in his pocket.

II

From then on, unconcerned with hunger and a lack of money, he lived with Coret in the decadent atelier, with Lebref the student, with me: – lost endlessly in idleness, love, strolls, music, cafés and moonlit nights with Erid. In hashish and cocaine ecstasies (which waiters in Montmartre supplied in exchange to good tips) he soon dreamed the most fabulous fusion of souls with her, an ecstatically intertwined future, halls erected, like the Eifel Tower, complete unity, the beauty of two beings; – soon he was once again befallen by doubt regarding the ideal just proclaimed, experimental projects of the most nervous suspense, fearful self-analyses and measurements using the self-constructed terrible inhumane scale. He was uninterested in our, his friends', most mundane, tangible socio-political debates about art. He did, however, convey (as never before) the exact wording of his bustling, urgent, muddled, even desperate conversations from these days with Erid. Thus erected, for him she almost embodied a marble image, more estranged day after day: – she no longer wanted to understand his fear, his insistence on the realization of the feeling of 'Thou-Being' experienced in the culmination of romantic-mystical ecstasy. Solitarily entangled in the mesh of Norwegian songs, creeping around with the decadent painter

Coret, with Lebref the student, to new ecstasies mendaciously woven around the pond bands; frequently even at home, nesting like little doves with their spouses (rediscovered in honour), pleasantly and softly sipping tea; indeed, often laughing amused and motherly over Gautier's avid struggle, yet often also princely incensed at the sudden but sometimes unintended destruction of the pitiful remnants of illusions caused by his more trenchant and severe, bold, explosively cast words: – in this way he became initially indifferent to her, then, recalcitrant, destructive, finally hostile.

And he, Gautier: sitting alone or (seldom) alienated, lost and distraught among us, with an almost accusatory voice, tediously recounting ridicule from his last meeting with Erid, here and there bringing up words like: Zerbinetta Ariadne! Narcissa! Psycho-prostitution! or: she 'internally' walks the streets! She is already together with another 'you there' again! The fusion failed due to a soul valve defect! ... – He gave up on the person, but still believed in the principle. And still this person, secretly apologizing again, greeting her on the street, occasionally even talking with her. – Then again dazed, cocaine-saturated, sunken, untouched by the others: – even by the suddenly approaching swirl of political complications that ravished the others of us on fulfilled evenings, the propulsive flow of people on the boulevards Montmartre and Poissonnière, illuminated telegrams, the departure of foreigners at Gare de L'est and Gare du Nord, the *Tricolore* suddenly storming on the streets, nightly torch-lit demonstrations in the flashing of the Eiffel Tower, mass speeches and singing in the sky basked in red.

III

By day: Place de la Concorde, circling up, boring into the blue of the endlessly high sky! Meadows and ponds undulate blossoming upwards, reflecting soul and stars: – consummated summer! – – – Then war was declared. – Cloud landscapes hectically and suddenly encamped on the horizon; odd, unnerving whooshing in street lights and trees along the boulevards; bewildered, gaunt faces blown around corners gave us a notion of multiply crossed-over muddled puddles of blood drifting down from hills burst open; a notion of the immense appearance of ships abruptly looming up (... shrieking fanfares over the ocean ...); notion of never beheld auras rising terribly upon forests and heights, resounding symphonies crouching by night in ghostly mountain passes (... twitching beams of light melting in blood and fire – finally! finally! – deeply intuited new monstrosity, Europe's torrid tiara full of pre-selected marvellous fraternity! ...) – recently still highly unlikely talons of presumably moribund militarism (Moloch now with swelling, all-consuming belly) enveloped us all. Coret the decadent painter, Lebref the student, Gautier Fémin and me ... And under the arch of whimpering grenades, hammer vortices of combat-shaken artillery in our backs, overlapped on both flanks by drum-hooves of English cavalry rushing forward (... 'en avant! en avant!' ...), it came to pass that Gautier Fémin, with strangely wind-blown countenance, gnashed at me 'En avant! en avant! – You are right a thousand times! – I'm not for this world! – My death is necessary! – Let's put an end to this!' – And while we broke into the grey phalanx of our enemies, beholding the lightning of the future striking our foreheads as well as theirs, one bullet (hallucinated, Norwegian) hit his. His deliberately exposed silhouette, reared up for a second, broke in the racket and roar – ejected from the European field. Gautier Fémin is dead!

* * *

But we strike out! En avant! En avant! We revolve around the fifteen fronts of the European nations: Aviators, crystalline spotlights, columns drumming in the sunrise! The most torn terrestrial Dionysus, we gather on the enormous city abutments of Europe's racing vaults –: hymns wrought from the darkness of the Dukla Pass, the ocean seething of the Skagerrak, the gases of Loos, the earthy blood of the banks of the Somme and the besmirched rubbish of Doberdò and Blackbird Field: – thus we stroll over your plains, Europe, like an illuminated whirlwind! New barricades are being constructed in the metropolises (… and again: the subways erupt and spray up! A train station floats in the air! …) rolled over by the ten-coloured banners, tied to the firmament of an endlessly desired, *desired* future! … We will return, the homeland of Europe above us, greeting the homeland from pole to pole. Resounding towers of Gothic cathedrals bow down, the bells swing, and quietly, swelling more and more, at last the high spirited song commences, song over buried death and life!!

(Dedicated to Felix Stiemer, in friendship)[2]

Originally published as 'Der Tod des Schwärmers Gautier Fémin', in *Das tönende Herz* (Dresden: Felix Stiemer Verlag, 1919).

NOTES

1. The city of Oslo was known as Kristiania from 1877-1925.

2. Felix Stiemer (1896-1945), important figure of the Dresden Expressionist scene, who, together with Rheiner, Felixmüller, Raoul Hausmann and others, founded the *Expressionistische Arbeitsgemeinschaft Dresden* (Dresden Expressionist Work Group). Stiemer subsequently established the Dresdner Verlag von 1917, and from 1917 published the journal *Menschen*, for which Rheiner was the editor from January to March 1919.

MIRAMÉE
(PARIS)

The calamity began in a crystalline summer night on the Boulevard Poissonnière. A woman sank to the ground in the pool of light cast by a street lamp; I caught her in my arms. It was Miramée. Her head lay on my shoulder. Like an island, her countenance surfaced divinely and softly out of the ether of her hair. A strange serenity rested in it as she opened her eyes for a moment and then slowly closed them again. It was as if the long boulevard had ceremoniously entered her with this gaze and vanished behind her sighing lips. She nestled her head closer to me, her hands softly clasping my arm, and she recovered slightly. 'Madame, you are not feeling well,' I said quietly. She whispered: 'Oh, I have suffered too much!'

I hailed a cab. As I helped her climb in and carried her weight for a moment, I felt how a great shared wave washed over both of us and disappeared in the current of trees and street lights.

The boulevard appeared very narrow and drew hectic images on the flowing window of our car. Miramée was sprawled on the upholstery. Occasionally a window, like a spot light, cast a bright cascade upon her lap. Her blue silk dress began to gleam. Her gaze hung on me indefinitely. Then came the moment in which I clearly understood that once before I had already seen, held, loved – must have loved her.

Where have we seen each other before?

Miramée, in the night we met straight across the terrible slumber of the metropolis and through the fog of people that glimmer in the night and voicelessly scream through the streets. *We were already tangled by merciless threads.* Our hands folded, and how sweet it is to dissolve in the sea and resound boundlessly through the seven rosy dawns!

Then we were in a large hotel close by the *Madeleine*, shadowy in a yellow room. A bed emerged black, was a threatening casket. The electric candelabra, an angry, red tumour, hung heavily over it. With a lost voice that sobbed along the walls she recounted her entire life, the macabre raging of her fate.

Should I sing you the song that came to me, this song that wrapped around the Eifel Tower and swirled in an unspeakable *vivace furioso*? … that circled and uncovered worlds of breathtaking dimensions? – Apaches of Montmartre, students of the Latin Quarter, Americans on tremendous ships and in screeching houses that in the evenings spout thousands of people and fountains of light, evenings glowing in the woods of Compiègne, terrible nights in sleazy and threatening hotels on the great boulevards, the flowing of the Seine under the misery of its grey bridges, a deep love full of fear and distress, stony doctors with sober findings, the hostile beds of the Salpêtrière Hospital, and through all of this, dreamt in hunger, the disturbing silhouette of the skinniest of all towers over Paris in an unfathomable glow of the morning sky: silver and lead, shimmering and dull …

I listened, listened carefully and slowly her small, unreal profile formed in me, as it must have so often occurred on the floating heights in the broad folds of the Sacré Coeur after a confession. Miramée descended upon Paris, her step pure and golden, a sweet cirrus cloud that came to us people and dissipated, dissipated in smoke and mire.

I remained in a reverie and enraptured for a long time. Then the here and now sneered at me again. Her body lay bare and white in bed, *which appeared to me as an endless sea, reverberating and primeval.* A pale sun swelled through the curtains coughing over the roofs of the Madeleine district. Savour her right breast. The left lay malignantly decayed and ulcerous, brown and full of malicious life. Her poor body was a grotto of rotting masses, painstakingly pieced and tied together. The right leg, black from the peeling skin, protruded into the air like a burnt stake. And all of these spots, upon which the terrible illness had fallen, glistened with a ghostly vitality. Decay nearly seemed to set in and the more it advanced the more it appeared to me as if a new being was arising there, giggling from her eye sockets and living in the teeth behind the dead, peeled-back lips.

I was gripped by a senseless fear. The bells began to chime, their wild tones scraped over me for a long time. Was it not those heavy syllables they slurred, slowly and grandly: 'MI-RA-MÉE, MI-RA-MÉE'? – Paris arose and bellowed at me. I stumbled out of the hotel like a maniac; I believed I saw fighting clamouring in the streets, *the Metro broke through the surface and came up, a train station floated in the air.*

I ran without a hat, without awareness.

I stopped in a suburb, exhausted on a bench. Then I lost consciousness. When I awoke they had brought me to a nearby tavern. There I was handed schnapps. The Parisian workers stood around me in their blue smocks and debated heatedly. Outside, on the Boulevard Ornano, the sun trembled, the sparrows chirped, and from the yard came the quiet singing of a small, unknowing maid:

> 'C'est une belle gosse,
> mais une sale rosse,
> on ne devrait jamais l'approcher.
> O quelle torture
> que l'on endure,
> quand on a le Malheur de l'aimer!'[1]

But I walked slowly and lightly, white roses in hand, down the Boulevard Ornano, out of Paris, into the boundless fields.

Originally published as 'Miramée', in *Die Aktion*, year 5, vol. 20/21 (Berlin, 1915), pp. 243-6, and then as part of Rheiner's collection *Der Bunte Tag*, Dichtung der Jüngsten, Vol. 12/13 (Dresden: Dresdner Verlag von 1917, 1919).

NOTE

1. The poem can be translated as follows:
   > She's a pretty lass,
   > But a pain in the ass,
   > One should never ever go near her.
   > Oh, what torture
   > One must endure,
   > should one have the misfortune to love her!

CABARET

The cabaret has huge name. Like a Berlin department store or a New York skyscraper. Even the scent of the Paris metro is perceptible to me when I hear the name '*Metropol Bierpalast*'. That is why I went there, with her, the very-beautiful, very-kind. Because it was still early we received wonderfully nice seats and were happy. The musicians lay around individually, incomplete on the stage like wax figures; they had not yet been put into service. Suddenly the headwaiter's belly darkened all views, causing me to slip into fear and trembling and scout for a policeman; this was because I did not consider it permissible. But he stood blithely stern at one of the doors; knew that his presence was so powerful that he could have been absent and yet still would have remained in control of the storm of visages, glasses and lights. Entities floated by in broad white or soft light collared blouses, billowing in the wind like sails. I regarded them as heavenly bats and their eyes looked very intelligent out from the lustre of their hair. The entire interior of the cabaret was fitted out in Japanese fashion and was called 'A Night in the Mikado Empire'. Large tableaus of Japanese men and women hung on the walls; they stood or sat around and looked at each other as if they wanted to commit indecent acts that very minute. Closer to the exit they actually did, but I only noticed this when leaving. The ceiling was covered with a cloud of paper lanterns and lampions. Several continually spun around as if driven by the gears of a clock. I later attributed their movement to the sweet progression of the orchestra music and the entire evening I was genuinely thankful for these paper lanterns that people could look up to as to the gods.

We drank beer. The quiet floating past of the white bats continued. All at once the orchestra burst into a brilliant chord. The director, dressed in a purple suit with tails, floated powerfully overhead. The contrabasses of the second Hungarian Rhapsody drew deep furrows in the crowd. Wine was being drunk at the next table; there was the jangle of change and glasses were clinked in a toast, while above them in the orchestra Frisca made poor Lassan crazy with her dances. I was very glad when it finally came to coitus: *tempo giusto*, ratatáh dadatatáh …

Then there was a small break during which the visitors' conversation hung on the Japanese ceiling like a swarm of mosquitos. The musicians cleared off the stage with surprising speed and disappeared completely into its backstage. The snow-white spotlights snapped on and spouted at them with unforgiving illumination. I closed my eyes softly in order to wait till the light had gathered enough strength to materialise a person on the stage. When I looked up again there stood a girl in a short kid's dress intended to evoke a ten-year-old, who with her bloody meat voice screamed out a song about prostitution in Vienna. Every word was a spittoon, every gesture professional bawdiness. She disappeared quickly because I removed my projection surface from her.

When I wanted to sit back down my gaze unexpectedly plunged into the cleavage of a lady sitting nearby. It remained lying there till the next number.

It was a gigantic Negress with an enormous, armoured chest. On the stage she grew like a tower. The conductor glittered with his diamonds and shimmered with his tails. She wore a fire-red dress with a train and her eyes were bushes in the jungle. She sang an English song with a beaming set of teeth and majestic gaze while her chin sloshed back and forth like a bulldog's. She performed as a vocal phenomenon; her voice was molten steel in the spout of the blast furnace; during the piano parts she circled over us like a tropical starry sky. She received much applause; even my little darling was shaken and clapped. Next she sang an American dance song. She did not dance during the refrain however, but merely hinted at the dance, which is perhaps the rage in all the saloons on the Bowery, with the syncopated twitching of her forearms and ankles. My heart leapt along.

Then she was gone. I saw her stride through the throng, enveloped in praise. She removed herself while her dress, fire red and becoming increasingly dark, followed with its train. And suddenly I was overcome by a dawning feeling, a notion of parting, and faces that had long remained in my soul appeared before me. I mentally embraced the woman next to me, who I loved, and for a moment I wanted to leave. But the music already offered an invitation.

It was very funny. The bandleader clowned around with his baton and the audience enjoyed itself greatly. There was turmoil inside of me. I was very close to the woman next to me, whom I loved. She talked and I listened. Sometimes I spoke as well but I never came across the thought of saying what was actually inside of me. A new row of white angels streamed silently past; they went to the bar. I was far away and the time probably lapsed. Once, when I looked up to the stage I caught sight of a droll Negro with a bass clarinet, with which he bellowed: '*Mariette, ma midinette*' ... His partner forbid him but he did it again and again. She played the *American girl* and was wearing very little. Her strong and firm breasts, over which the dress was stretched, rolled around in my head so that I thought the dress would burst, but that did not occur.

A humourist came, sang, told tales and did capers. We both laughed a lot. Then we left. Under the door the conductor wound up powerfully one last time; but the Japanese images, which had already moved on to greater bawdiness, turned their backs on us. The lanterns danced, the music screeched, the bosoms glowed. – What remained was the face of the coat check girl, poor, distant, sober and insistent. *Was she the one I later held in my arms, in the hot, boundless night?*

Originally published as 'Kabarett' in: *Der Bunte Tag*, Dichtung der Jüngsten, Vol. 12/13 (Dresden: Dresdner Verlag von 1917, 1919).

NOCTURNE

(COLOGNE)

I walk past the cathedral. There it stands: unquenchable, clawing into the night with a great gesture ...

Soft little cocottes stand in the shadow of the houses with a mouth twitch oh so familiar to me when a large bloated man pussyfoots up to one of them and touches her breast with wide frog fingers.

And I stand in the train station.

There a brown train, which at night howls its distress from London via Ostend, Berlin and Warsaw to Moscow, rests on the rails, breathing like an anguished animal.

And I know: –

Around this time heavy clouds of snow sink deep in the Canadian woods;

Around this time a sick, tired octopus rolls across the ocean floor towards death;

Around this time another mouldering landscape crumbles from the aged moon. –

And I know: –

I perceive all of this: the deep misery in which I lay, the bright happiness in which I fly in other hours;

within me is the fear of the beaver; the hunger of the kangaroo jumping isolated under southern stars; my soul is an enclosure full of wild animals, full of lurking, angry monkeys and gnawing hyenas;

and I am powerless, poor; I fall down before it like a naked savage who, in a hot daze and dark broiling swamps, hears the ball lightning rolling around the Kilimanjaro; – and yet I cry and laugh and sing with cracked lips;

and my heart glows like a pearl, and my eyes are diamonds: –

My world! My great, dancing world!

Originally published as 'Nocturne', in *Der Bunte Tag*, Dichtung der Jüngsten, Vol. 12/13 (Dresden: Dresdner Verlag von 1917, 1919).

ARRIVAL

The muffled station in the summer night
bellows like an animal. In the spacious hall
a thousand people stand silent and dark, all,
and as if led to slaughter, closed up tight.

And how the trains with clanging squalls
enter in evil's embodied delight,
a black sun is resuscitated bright
and hangs in the sky, close, as if in fall.

– And within me heavy, without a fight,
arises a terrible chill – spreads with gall
its claws as if a bat before the light.

The darkness blazes anew a boundless wall.
And bursting my heart wells up from its fright, –
– becomes roaring large, an avalanche ball.

Originally published as 'Ankunft', in *Der bunte Tag*, Dichtung der Jüngsten
(Dresden: Dresdner Verlag von 1917, 1919).

PRAYER IN THE WAR

You who roars in the canons' drone
and in deeply puzzled glances
sometimes shows a merely darting face;

guest with corpses that silently throne
upon the hill, far from the dance,
panting light's lamenting maze;

you who wanders in the trenches,
lingering, tearstained, without purpose,
creeps around fire in choking gloom:

Grant us, pale in deaths' beastly clenches,
dull and hungry, what we yearn for;
show us your hands, their radiant wounds!

We are often crucified and our plight
soaked by cursed vinegar and gall;
motionless in the bayonets' mean fight,
our bodies wedged in a bloody wall.

Rise up through the blustery heights,
that hang over our empty skulls.
Make us free, you: prince of peace and knight,

Raiser of the dead! Heavenly gift!!

(For René Schickele)[1]

Originally published as 'Gebet des Christen im Krieg' in *Die weissen Blätter*, year 3 (Leipzig, 1916), p.16; and subsequently as 'Gebet im Krieg', in: *Das Schmerzliche Meer: frühe und neue Gedichte* (Dresden: Dresdner Verlag von 1917, 1918).

NOTE

1. René Schickele (1883-1940): German-French writer, essayist and translator, and publisher of *Die weissen Blätter*.

MAGICAL SONG

I am a human – I am afraid.
I fear the black clouds,
they: iron ringing on the dead border of the sky!
And I avoid house walls,
the silent doors frighten me;
sparkling handle, how fateful it touches my
        hand!

Overwhelmed by grey and shivering
soil, under God's cold blows and murderous stabs
– a human!, what shadows of great, inevitable
        events!
I am afraid, I am terrified,
built, steered by the mystery word and magical line,
powerfully encircled by stars and storm and unfathomable
        one times one!

In the flash of the near sun at morning,
and in the bottomless gloaming of the portentous heart
I recognise myself and you, all of us, in our anguished being!
That which stalked us from the inception,
the creature, predator – God!, I feel revulsion!

How we are captured, buried and covered up by night
        and wind!

I feel, observe! – I am human.
I fear my observations;
Oh, bloody quaking under stars! Oh, great scrutiny of the heart!
My step, my sound, my deepest sleep, my breath and
        tone of pulse.
My girl, my child. Oh, silence! Oh, great, inaudible
        path of the earth!
I am a human. I do not fear! I love destiny!

Unpublished poem entitled 'Magischer Gesang', signed 'Cologne, 2-7-21,
18.00 o'clock in the evening' (= 2nd of July 1921), manuscript in the Walter
Rheiner Archive at the Akademie der Künste, Berlin.

NIGHT AND DREAM

We traversed all foreign cities,
and distance radiates from our coats.
The buildings burn palely into our skin.
Trees and street lights, entangled twisted thorns
around our blue and star-enveloped brains.

The great sickness grips us angrily,
Leaves boundless space in our breast;
and around the candle feverishly
swirling it throws us to the bed, void, dead.

Yet outside the smoke of the terrible night!
The earth's rotation resounds through it.
On oceans ships reel helplessly stark
like stiffened carcasses, full of people,

commemorating their brothers,
in gigantic houses in the country
that burns under the unforgiving sun
tumorous and always festering fierce. –

At this hour in Berlin the elevated
railway shoots light blossoms up in the air;
full of people commemorating their
brothers, who are now on the Cape of Good Hope
and in the Table Mountain's lunar blue
see flying dogs and hyenas.

Swimming cities on the Yellow River:
Myriads of Chinese swirl after them.
An opaque star is near to our planet.
The river reverses and turns uphill.

We all drift in the river, all of us.
Don't we discern ourselves through flood and tang?
In the negro's mouth? In the red man's crest? –
– And don't the planets look upon us with
telescopes, commemorating brothers? –

Are we rotting? The night is always there!
Sweetly we sink in nameless velveteen.
Already our shadows haunt the rooftops.
A grey and pointless day knocks on the window.

The moon, this yellow eye stares upon us
and roams back and forth like a carnivore:
the people, hypnotically entwined
with it, hang out from chimneys, corpse-like.

Embellishments creep through our dead bodies,
from a woman who possesses our souls.

The silent bed stands tranquil in the street
and miserable people say 'good morning'.
My dead father floats in my direction:
he gives me money, he loves me and he laughs;
yet my mother sits disgruntled, hard,
doesn't fathom me and wanes on asphalt.

Through thousands of spheres, large in blue and gold
The Lord *God* vibrates in my earthly heart;
His backbone clings to the ground
and aches, and his eyes are so very ill.

Dreamt images take flight with cries.
A woman's toothless brown mouth steams;
a thousand years old and swaying slightly,
camels saunter over her desert brain.

And the Nile streams great into our hearts.
Now we are sea, are sand, are hazy stars.
The earth continues; the pale ball floats up there.
We are substance and ether. Who forms us?

(for my dead father)

Originally published as 'Nacht und Traum', in: *Mythische Insel*; reprinted in *Das Schmerzliche Meer* (Dresden: Dresdner Verlag von 1917, 1918).

END

I have buried my dream, kissed my blood one last
       time,
– I, between darkness and black fires,
       striding.
My head is heavy, and my heart deeply besotted.

A forest, a singing forest froze; a bright ship sank
       in silence.
The songbirds die, and the ice creeps into the room, into
       the breast.
And no sun shines, no star! – The skies stare
       dead. –

How cold I am! My woman is far away, I hardly know
the faces of my children anymore. The lock I long wore,
– a relic – is stiff and strange.

– So I retch my empty heart, which ghosts plundered
       from me.
I close my eyes. I lean my forehead in the depth of the last
       night.

It will be a cold girlfriend for me, as on the streets whores
       and dogs,
roaming around windy corners, – a last mild comforter …

Originally published as 'Ende', in: *Das Fo-Buch* (Dresden: Rudolf Kaemmerer Verlag, 1921).

'COME, GENTLE SNOW!'

Come, gentle snow! Blanket this heavy heart!
With your grace and magic freeze the tears,
that flow from the eternal source,
born daily, loved evermore.

Oh, grant that from this lost and bitter suffering,
becomes the great, the serious grave
wherein I will find myself at peace:
weeping, lovingly redeemed soul.

This untitled and unpublished, signed 'Written on May 10, 1925, at half past six in the evening', is Rheiner's last known work. Manuscript in the Walter Rheiner Archive at the Akademie der Künste, Berlin.

Walter Rheiner, around 1920.

A morphine prescription
dated 15-8-1920, likely
forged by Rheiner (courtesy
Akademie der Künste, Berlin,
Walter Rheiner Archive, nr 37).

Front-page of the journal *Menschen,* 15 January 1919, edited by Rheiner.

The grave of Walter Rheiner at the Kaiser-Wilhem-Gedächtnis-Friedhof in Berlin (source: Wikicommons. Von Genealogist – Eigenes Werk, CC BY-SA 3.0, https://commons.wikimedia.org/w/index.php?curid=25407560).

KOKAIN

KOKAIN

I

Nacht hing groß in den Bäumen der Allee und tropfte auf seine Schultern nieder, da Tobias unter den flüsternden Ästen dahinschritt. Er ging und ging, die Allee hinauf und hinab, fast schon zwei Stunden lang.

Die Normaluhr (ehernes Gespenst an der Straßenkreuzung) zeigte schon halb elf. Im Sterben dieses Sommerabends, der in unzähligen allerzartesten Tinten hinter dem Riesenrumpf der ewigen grauen Gedächtniskirche zerfloß, war Tobias aufgebrochen – ergriffen von jener düsteren Unruhe, die immer wiederkam und ihn desto mehr quälte, je mehr er ihr zu entfliehen oder sie zu betäuben suchte im Trubel des klirrenden Cafés, jener armseligen Stube mit den roten Plüschsesseln und den grinsenden Fratzen kaltblütiger Gäste, die dort ein unwirkliches Leben führten – ein Dasein von bunten Abziehbildchen, wie sie uns als Kindern geschenkt werden. Wie oft, so auch diesmal war er dort hingeflohen vor dem Zergehen der sommerlichen Sonne, das weich über den nahen Himmel rann und seine Unruhe zum Irrsinn zu steigern drohte.

Und doch siegte immer diese Unruhe, die, wenn sie kam, ihm alle Räume verhaßt machte – sein chambre garnie so gut wie das Café oder den großen Raum der Straßen und Plätze. Aufgescheucht war er gegangen, als der Abend schon (dunkler Strom) blau über die Häupter der Passanten ausgegossen war. Jetzt war die Nacht da. Flimmernd strahlte der Asphalt auf, wenn ein Automobil surrend an Tobias vorbeistob. Aus den Café-Vorgärten schwemmte eine süße Musik über ihn hin. Gesprächsfetzen wehten, ungehört von ihm, vorüber. Es war ein stetes Wandeln bunter, vornehmer Damen, diskreter Herren da, ein unaufhörlicher Verkehr lachender Equipagen und Autos, der melancholisch-heitere Abendgesang der großen düsteren Stadt, die auf ihre Art zu leben verstand.

… Und er? Verstand er zu leben? Wie lebte er denn?

Geblendet stand er an der Schwelle des Platzes, und eine

Fontäne von Licht und Lauten umsprang ihn. Er sann nach, kurz, abrupt.

Gewiß kein Leben dieser Art, das ebenso Schein ist wie die bunten Roben, die strahlenden Autos, die lächelnden Masken, die ihm vorüberzogen. Wie lebte er? Was war dies: das Aufstehen morgens um zehn oder elf Uhr, manchmal auch mittags; dies Aufstehen mit dem tiefen Ekel vor seinem Zimmer, vor seinen Büchern, seinen Kleidern, seiner eigenen Person? Die tägliche Konstatierung, dass er kein Geld habe, und dies Überlegen, woher er es bekommen könne, von welchem Bekannten oder Unbekannten und durch welche Mittel. Dieser tägliche Hunger gleich morgens, den er verachtete. Die tägliche Abwehr gegen die alte Zimmerwirtin, die ihre Miete verlangte. Dann dies lustlose Verlassen des Hauses, das ihm ebenso zuwider war wie die unendlich lange Straße, in der es stand und die den höhnischen Namen des großen Philosophen führte, dessen Werke er einst gelesen hatte und der ihm wie ein Vater erschien, der mit dem Krückstock drohte. Das schlechte Gewissen, mit dem er um Geld bat im Café oder vor den Sesseln der Redakteure, die ihm erstaunt den Zigarrenrauch ins Gesicht bliesen und ihn verdrießlich abschüttelten. Diese Leere des Hirns, das ekelhafte Ressentiment, das er spürte und das ihn ungerecht machte gegen alle Leute mit anständigen Anzügen, zufriedenem Antlitz und ruhigem Schritt. Und dann: – dann kam der große Fluch, der Abend, der ihn einspann und die dämonische Unruhe brachte, die ihn wie einen Kreisel sich um sich selbst drehen ließ. *Die Vöglein pfiffen* – und unentrinnbar stand er seinem Schicksal gegenüber, das sich vor ihm aufbaute und ihm mit mächtiger Hand seinen Weg wies: Geh!

So ging er. Er ging alle Tage, vorgestern und gestern und heute. *Entrinnen gab es nicht.* Den Tod später oder vielleicht, *hoffentlich*, gelegentlich als zufällige Konsequenz. Er ging. Und richtig: da war die Stelle! Er war, wie immer, richtig stehengeblieben.

Nachtglocke zur Apotheke. Also geschellt und warten.

Da wurde das Licht entzündet, das Klapptürchen ging auf. Der Apotheker streckte den kahlen Kopf heraus.

»Herr Doktor ...«

»Na, schon wieder da? ... Können Sie denn nicht eher kommen?«

»Bitte um Entschuldigung, ich hatte...«

Aber die Glatze war schon fort.

Ja, was hatte er? Er hatte gekämpft wie fast jeden Abend und war, wie immer, unterlegen. Ein großes Achselzucken über die ganze Welt!

Der Apotheker erschien wieder: »Drei Mark fünfzig.«

Tobias murmelte: »So viel habe ich nicht.«

»Na, gut«, sagte der Apotheker, »ich werd's noch mal aufschreiben, aber wehe, wenn Sie nicht zahlen: Sie wissen ja!«

»Danke schön«, flüsterte Tobias. »Guten Abend.«

Nun war kein Sinnen mehr und keine Gedanken, keine Sorge und keine Frage, da er das ewige Gift in den Händen hielt, die sich wie zum Gebet um die kleine sechseckige Flasche falteten. Er selbst war jetzt das Leben, und sein Herz übertönte die Welt!

Im Café, auf der Toilette, gab er sich drei Injektionen hintereinander, verschloß Flasche und Injektionsspritze wieder sorgfältig und steckte alles in die Hosentasche.

Nun fühlte er sich frei und leicht, spielerisch, ein junger Gott! Strahlend betrat er das Café und lächelte den jungen Frauen, rümpfte die Nase über die eleganten Kavaliere.

Ein Wink von ihm, und er würde, Ikarus, dem göttlichen Jüngling gleich, lächelnd an die Decke schweben, singend über den Baldachin des Vorgartens gleiten und auf zu den knisternden Sternen kreisen.

II

Federnden Schrittes ging er hin und ließ sich am beglänzten Marmortisch voll plaudernder Frauen und Herren nieder. Er bestellte und entzündete die herbe Zigarette, den Gefährten in Trauer und Glück.

Doch da er aufschaute, *sah er die Nacht drohen* hinter dem aromatischen Qualm, den sein Mund ausstieß – *jene Nacht, seine Nacht, die mit schwarzem Faustschlag diese kurzen Minuten des heiteren Rausches zertrümmerte* und sich selbst unerbittlich heranschob mit jenem *neuen düsteren Qual-Rausch, dessen rhapsodischen Gesang, endlos gedehnt, sie ihm von jetzt an in die Ohren gellte.*

Was verzerrten sich die Antlitze ihm gegenüber am Tisch, die eben noch lächelten? Woher die schielende Bedeutung in den Blicken, die diese Menschen ihm zuwarfen und dann untereinander austauschten, vielsagend und unwillig?

Und da beugten sie sich auch schon zueinander und flüsterten …

Angestrengt horchte er hin … und da, war es nicht da? Hatte er nicht eben deutlich das Wort vernommen, das fatale Wort, das riesenhaft über die Firmamente dieser seiner Nächte gespannt war und (im Klang schon erbarmungslose Maschine) ihn langsam zerhackte: – *Kokain! … Ko-ka-in!*

Stück für Stück hackte es ab von ihm, bis er dereinst bald ganz zermalmt sein wird.

Da, jener Herr (… bleich sprang Tobias der Schreck in die Augen …): ganz deutlich, unerhört leise und klar zugleich, hatte er gesagt: »Diese Bestie pumpt sich jeden Abend mit Kokain voll!«

Ach, da schlug das Herz in rasendem Getrommel, da würgte etwas den kalten klammen Hals, da fuhr eine geisterhafte Hand durch das Haar, das zitterte, und ein kalter Schweiß brach über dem Rückgrat aus.

Auf! Fort von hier! *Schon schwirrte die große Peitsche in der Luft über seinem Haupt. Es knallte und klatschte laut.* Bebend bezahlte er, erhob sich wankend und wie gelähmt und floh, floh aus diesem Kessel hinaus.

Ein Blick zurück im Hinausstürzen zeigte ihm noch, wie alles Publikum schon aufmerksam geworden war. Man lachte, man deutete auf Tobias.

Ein fetter Herr, ganz rot im Gesicht, schlug sich brüllend vor Lachen auf den Schenkel und bog sich zurück, der rote Kopf drohte abzubrechen und hinter die Stuhllehne zu kollern. – Gräßlich! – Die Wirbeltür spie Tobias auf die Straße. Aber auch hier war kein Rasten für ihn.

Die Menschen blieben stehen und schauten ihn an. Harmlose Spaziergänger schüttelten die Köpfe und ließen Tobias herankommen, um ihn genauer zu betrachten. Hier konnte er nicht bleiben!

Er drückte sich eilig die Häuser entlang, die Joachimsthaler Straße hinauf, zum Bahnhof: schon gehetztes Wild, verscheucht von jedem Fensterladen, der sein Licht auf ihn warf.

Was blieb ihm übrig in solcher Not, *da Gott ihn höhnisch auf den nächtigen Wolken anschrie und Erzengel eherne Fäuste schüttelten, daß die Straßen klirrend widerhallten?*

Was blieb anderes als das gebenedeite Gift, das er in der Tasche trug?

Die Tränen stiegen ihm bereits in die Kehle, als er in der Bahnhofshalle verschwand. Wieder kehrte er ein bei den Aborten, er, der stete Gast, er, *die stinkende Kellerassel, das Klärichtvieh.*

Hei, *da pfiffen, den lieben Vöglein auf der Dämmerung gleich,* die Bahnhofsbeamten auf ihren Signalpfeifen – oh, da klappten die Schaltertürchen der Fahrkartenausgabe auf, und alles schaute diesem Menschen nach, der, einem Betrunkenen ähnlich, zu den Aborten torkelte.

Er riegelte sich auf einem der Klosetts ein. Was war das für ein Leben? Ein Aasleben! O du verhaßt-geliebtes Gift, Kokain, Kokain (... die Maschine stampfte: klick-klack, klick-klack: wieder ein Stück ab ...).

Oben donnerte der Zug in die Halle (... sicherlich, dachte Tobias, Expreß zur Riviera, weiß schon: blaue Gestade, taubenumflattert, Pinien- und Orangenhain und der selige Berg: Santa Margherita ...), und er nahm zwei neue Injektionen vor, in beide Oberschenkel je eine.

Das erleichterte einen Augenblick: ... Riviera, dachte Tobias, Riviera, Santa Margherita ...

Dann betete er, murmelnd: *Gib, lieber Herr von Gott, du selige Exzellenz, gib, daß ich bei der nächsten Injektion lautlos verrecke!*

Als er die Waschräume der Bahnhofshalle verließ, schien ein Rauschen den riesigen gewölbten Raum zu erschüttern. Normaluhr drohte mit aufrechtem Finger: zwölf Uhr.

In der Vorhalle war ein tosender Verkehr. Gekreisch einer Horde von Satanen stürzte in Tobias' Ohren, der sich durch die (vermeintliche) Menschenmenge drängte, schamerfüllt, als sei er nackt.

Hatten diese Menschen, dieses Gebräu aus Hohn und Schadenfreude, nichts anderes zu tun, als ihm aufzulauern, sich am Bahnhof aufzustellen um Mitternacht, um dies Schauspiel zu genießen: – wie er, der Kokainist, aus seiner Kloake gekrochen kam, mit blutenden Armen und Beinen, an die sich das Hemd festklebte? Fluch über sie! Fluch über seinen hellen Anzug ... Da: waren das nicht schon Blutflecke?

Er feuchtete die Fingerspitzen an und wollte so die Flecken fortreiben.

Am Ausgang wollte er sich in die Brandung der Straße stürzen, doch plötzlich schwenkte er ab und versteckte sich unter der Bahnüberführung.

III

Zwei Damen standen an der Straßenecke, dem Bahnhofsausgang gegenüber. Tobias äugte schnaufend hin: Oh, wie kamen die hierher?

Das war seine Mutter und seine Schwester. Aber waren die nicht in Köln?

Gewiß, die mußten eigentlich in Köln sein! Aber wer weiß? Vielleicht hatte sie der Herr Bahnhofsvorsteher telegraphisch nach Berlin gerufen, damit die Mutter ihren Sohn, die Schwester ihren Bruder sehen könne, teilnehmen könne an dem unterhaltenden Schauspiel, das das Publikum von Berlin W allabendlich genoß, interessanter und billiger als im Palast-Theater oder in Nelsons Künstlerspielen, an der amüsanten

Tragikomödie: *»Der Kloakenprinz«* oder: *»Mein Gott, mein Gott, warum hast du mich verlassen.«*

Sie standen an der Ecke, im brutalen Licht der bläulichen Bogenlampe. Die Kleider wehten ihnen um die Leiber. Es war ein Klappern da, als ob ihnen die Gebeine schlotterten. *Oder waren es seine?* Seine Knie zitterten. Die Hände auch. *Sie waren so dünn!* Sah er durch die gespreizten Finger hindurch, so waren die vielen Lichter wirr gaukelnde kalte Monde, die mit leisem Puff von den schwarzen Pfählen sprangen und auf dem Asphalt zerschellten.

Regungslos standen die beiden Frauenfiguren. Ha, er kannte das! … sie taten so unbeteiligt und hielten ihn doch scharf im Auge! …

Kleine blonde Schwester, lieber Dotz, warum läßt du mir keine Ruhe? Und Sie, Frau Sch…, Eveline oder Ernestine mit– dem schwer aussprechlichen Vatersnamen, Sie, teure Mutter, wie? … mir schon wieder auf den Fersen? Und so weit her! Vom Rande Deutschlands« nach Berlin, bloß um den Verlorenen Sohn zu ängstigen? Würdig, dreimal würdig Ihrer Mutterliebe! … Was steht ihr da? Wie? Ihr Grimassen!

Eine Welle flog durch sein brausendes Gehirn. Er faßte sich ein Herz. Wut packte ihn.

Er ging auf die beiden Gestalten zu, wollte am Ausgange des Untergrundbahnhofes vorbei, der seine Treppe auf die Straße warf, von stilisierten Lampen umrankt.

Aber es quoll aus dem Schlund des unterirdischen Baues herauf – eine schwarze Menschenmenge, die ihn rasch umzingelte. Geschrei ohrfeigte ihn aufs neue. Schnell atmend entwand er sich dieser neuen Gefahr und schoß auf die Straßenecke zu, wo die beiden Damen standen.

Standen? Standen?

Er sah nur zwei Reklameschilder, in Schwarz und Gold, die ihm unverschämt entgegenleuchteten. Keine Frauen da, kein Mensch! ... Ach, ein kümmerlicher Hund nur strich langsam um die Ecke, schnüffelte und verrichtete seine übliche Notdurft.

Tobias, der seine Lunge dunkel, schwer und wie samten werden fühlte, drückte sich in den Hauseingang und spritzte, halbtot vor Angst, beobachtet zu werden, ein neues Quantum Kokain in den rasch vom Ärmel entblößten Unterarm.

IV

Ja, siehe, da standen die bebenden Sterne wieder still, einen Augenblick lang. – Heiliges Gift! Heiliges Gift! – Das fühlte Tobias und sah den Dämon, der ihm ebenso vertraut wie schrecklich war, weit über dem nächtigen Himmel stehen. Er wußte und flüsterte es ins Firmament hinauf: *»Du bist der Tod, die Gnade und das Leben. Du hast keinen Gott neben dir!«*

Er ging die Straße wieder hinab.

An der Kreuzung des Kurfürstendamm betrat er die grün erleuchtete Rotunde. Ein älterer Herr war darin und ordnete seine Kleider, als Tobias sich an ein Abteil stellte und Vorbereitungen traf, um zu urinieren.

Tobias fühlte sich beobachtet. Seine Hände flogen ratlos an seinem Anzug hin und her. Er konnte keinen Augenblick still stehen, er wandte sich um, wechselte das Abteil, befühlte alle Taschen seines Anzugs, tastete nach Flasche und Spritze und schaute schließlich ratlos in die Augen des Herrn, der lange fertig zum Fortgehen war und ihn aufmerksam und mit kalter Ruhe betrachtete.

Schließlich ging er und ließ Tobias in heller Verzweiflung zurück … Um Gottes willen! Das war ein Detektiv, ein Sanitätsbeamter, ein Abgesandter der Mutter, der er vorhin begegnet war und die sich vor ihm verbarg!

Minutenlang stand Tobias ratlos in diesem achteckigen übelriechenden Raum, an dessen Wänden ein schleimiges Wasser niederrann und von Zeit zu Zeit plötzlich aufzischte, als wolle es ihn angeifern.

Gewißlich standen sie jetzt draußen im Kreis um die Rotunde, ein schweigender Kordon. Handschellen klirrten, Zwangsjacke war zum Überwerfen bereit. Ein Schluchzen würgte Tobias' Kehle, die beizend trocken war. Durst! Durst! … In letzter Wirrnis zu allem entschlossen, verließ er schließlich die Bude und wankte ins Freie hinaus.

Er war sehr erstaunt, niemand vorzufinden, der auf ihn lauerte.

Doch da (… jäher Schreck schraubte ihm die Augen in den Kopf …) da stand der alte Herr und pfiff. Pfiff laut, einmal, zweimal!

Halt! Halt! – Tobias rannte auf ihn zu, zog schlotternd den Hut und sprach ihn atemlos an: »Sie müssen sich nicht wundern, Herr, daß ich so aufgeregt bin! Ich habe ein schreckliches Erlebnis hinter mir! Ich versichere Ihnen, wirklich, glauben Sie mir: *ich bin nicht wahnsinnig! Noch nicht!* Auch nicht betrunken oder vergiftet! Glauben Sie mir! Pfeifen Sie nicht Ihren Leuten! Lassen Sie mich gehen!«

Verwundert maß ihn der Herr vom Kopf bis zu den Füßen. Er trat einen Schritt zurück und sagte: »Wie meinen Sie? Ich verstehe Sie nicht. Was gehen Sie mich denn an? Ich pfeife meinem Hunde.«

Er pfiff wieder. Da kam ein dunkler Schäferhund gelaufen, schweifwedelnd sprang er auf seinen Herrn zu.

»Entschuldigen Sie«, murmelte Tobias und zog sich schnell zurück. Sicherlich war das eine Falle! Oh, er hatte das heimliche Blinken in den Augen des Herrn gesehen! Hier galt es, sich in Sicherheit zu bringen.

Tobias wandte sich zur Kaiserallee und rannte ein Stück unter den Bäumen, bis ihm die Brust zu bersten drohte. Er blieb stehen und sah sich um. Tiefe Nacht und kein Mensch zu sehen. Die Normaluhr zeigte halb eins.

V

Hier, im Schatten des Gebüschs, nahm er sein Jackett ab, legte es auf das Pflaster an einen Baumstamm, krempelte den Hemdsärmel auf, der große dunkle Blutlachen zeigte und den eigentümlichen Geruch vergossenen Blutes ausströmte, und nahm, mit knirschend zusammengebissenen Zähnen, in aller Sorgfalt und mit betonter Langsamkeit, zwei Injektionen vor.

Er hielt die Flasche gegen das ferne Laternenlicht. Sie war noch zu zwei Dritteln voll. Befriedigt schob er sie in die Hosentasche, zog die andere Flasche hervor und wusch den Oberarm mit Äther ab. Auch Stirn und Hals netzte er damit.

Die Büsche in den Vorgärten flüsterten. In der Ferne nahte eine der letzten Straßenbahnen.

Rasch zog Tobias sich wieder an.

Oh, nun wünschte er zu Hause zu sein, um die Verderbnis, hinter verriegelten und verhangenen Schlössern, ganz auszukosten. Nach seinem möblierten Zimmer aber, das wußte er, konnte er nicht gehen. Die Wirtin würde seine Zimmertür abgeschlossen und den Schlüssel fortgesteckt haben, so daß er nicht hinein können wird.

Wohin, wohin, mein Gott, in seiner Not! Barhäuptig stand er unter den Sternen.

Sollte er wiederum, wie öfter schon, die ganze Nacht herumirren, um schließlich den grauen Morgen am Spreekanal zu finden oder an der Gasanstalt, die dann wie eine Faust aus den Nebeln stiege?

Der Äther mußte irgendwie die rasende Erregung gemindert haben, die ihn gefangenhielt. Sein Puls, das fühlte er, ging noch fliegend, hoch, schnell. Oder war es das Alleinsein, die Abwesenheit von Menschen, die ihm diese relative Ruhe gab?

Er setzte sich in Marsch, mit der Zähigkeit des Gift-Fanatikers, die ihn nicht Muskeln noch Sehnen spüren ließ. Die lange Kaiserallee hinab bis zum Bahnhof Wilmersdorf-Friedenau. Hier schwenkte er seitlich ab und stand bald vor dem großen Mietshaus.

Hier wohnte Marion, die goldene Freundin aus dem Café, in einem großen Atelier.

Die Haustür war verschlossen. Er pfiff einige Male und rief: »Marion, Marion!«

Vergeblich. Sicherlich schlief sie schon.

Während er wartend auf und ab ging und die Nachtluft aus dem freien Vorstadtgelände ihn umwehte, begann aufs neue der schwarze Himmel auf ihm zu lasten. Die Sterne tropften schwer und klebrig. Die hohen Häuser bedrückten ihn. Der Wind sang in den schwingenden Bogenlampen, die ein irres und grelles Licht umherwarfen.

Die Angst befiel ihn aufs neue. Er sah sich furchtsam um, schlich in einen dunklen Winkel und verabreichte sich zwei neue Spritzen.

Ha, da schoß das Fieber, gäle Flamme, wieder in ihm auf! Die Stirn knisterte, die Augen wurden weit und paralytisch aufgezerrt. Ruhelos trat er von einem Bein aufs andere.

Fast hatte er schon vergessen, was er hier wollte, als sich Schritte dem Hause näherten.

Ein Herr blieb vor der Haustür stehen und rasselte mit seinen Schlüsseln.

Tobias trat schüchtern hinzu und grüßte.

»Es öffnet niemand«, sagte er stockend, »ich soll eine Dame zu ihrer kranken Verwandten holen.«

Der Herr ließ ihn schweigend durch die geöffnete Tür und schloß wieder ab.

Tobias schaltete das Minutenlicht ein und rannte in großer Eile die Treppen hinauf.

Plötzlich fiel ihm ein, daß es besser sei, den Herrn erst in seine Wohnung gehen zu lassen. Er wartete. Schon im ersten Stock öffnete der Angekommene eine Flurtür und trat ein. Die Tür fiel zu. Das Licht erlosch. Durch die bunten Glasfenster des Treppenhauses drang phantastisch das zitternde Licht der Laternen von unten herauf.

Tobias schlich zagend zum vierten Stock empor, mit tödlicher Angst vor jedem Treppenabsatz, der ihn an einer Wohnung vorbeiführte.

Oben, im vierten Stock, führte erst eine angelehnte Tür in einen korridorartigen Vorraum mit Lichtschachtfenster. Im Hintergrunde war eine schwere Eisentür, die zu Marions Atelier ging.

Wieder schaltete Tobias das Licht ein. Auf das Fensterbrett des Lichtschachtes stellte er seine Flasche und das Etui mit seiner Injektionsspritze. Er rieb wieder die blutigen Arme mit Äther ab und genoß eine neue Einspritzung.

Da begannen mit Macht neue Halluzinationen.

Er fuhr herum. Unten im Treppenhaus, im Erdgeschoß, erhoben sich Stimmen, Stimmen vieler Menschen, die sich anschickten emporzusteigen. Ein wirres, halblautes Geflüster. Tobias unterschied einzelne Perioden: *»Das muß endlich aufhören ... Es ist ein Skandal ... Das Schwein ruiniert sich und seine Angehörigen ... Ins Irrenhaus mit dem Subjekt! ... Wir werden ihn ins Automobil schaffen ... Packen Sie ihn nur gleich! ... Und daß er nicht die Flasche austrinkt, das bringt der Kerl fertig ...«*

Tobias zitterte. Schweiß rann ihm (... oder war es Blut?). Er hörte die Stimme seiner Mutter, während das Licht wieder erlosch: *»Tobias, mein Sohn! Tobias, ich flehe dich an! ... Tobias, Tobias! ... Tobias ...«*

Die Stimme verhallte klagend. Tapp, tapp, tapp! Man stieg die Treppen herauf, regelmäßig, immer näher. Das Geflüster zwischendurch verstummte keinen Augenblick.

Sollte er es wagen, das Licht wieder anzuzünden? ... Er tat's.

... Da lag vor ihm, vor seinen Füßen, leise sich noch windend, der Körper der sterbenden Mutter. Daneben hockte schwarz gekleidet, das Gesicht in schwarze Schleier gehüllt, die Schwester und weinte leise, gesenkten Hauptes.

Tobias fuhr zurück. Er wandte sich ab und preßte das heiße Gesicht an die Wand.

VI

Das Herz klopfte wie ein Hammer an seine Schädeldecke. Nach einer Weile wandte er sich um. Der Spuk war verschwunden. Schnell nahm er eine neue Spritze und begann, erst leise, dann lauter und lauter, an die Eisentür zu klopfen.

Er beugte sich zum Schlüsselloch nieder und rief »Marion! Marion!« mit unterdrückter Stimme hinein. Zwischendurch fuhr er alle Augenblicke herum, damit ihn niemand rücklings ergreife.

Endlich sah er durch das Schlüsselloch, daß drinnen Licht entstand. Ein Schatten bewegte sich auf dem Fußboden und näherte sich der Tür. Eine dünne, verschlafene Stimme, Marions Stimme, fragte angstvoll: »Wer ist da, um Gottes willen?«

»Ich bin's, ich, Tobias … Marion, mach auf, ich muß hinein.«

Die Tür wurde geöffnet und kreischte leise in den Angeln. Tobias, dem durch die letzten, schnell aufeinanderfolgenden Einspritzungen ein wilder Paroxysmus im Körper wühlte, torkelte hinein.

Marion, im Nachtgewand, stand vor ihm, eine Kerze in der Hand. Sie kannte Tobias und seinen Zustand, denn nicht zum ersten Male suchte er sie in der Nacht auf. –

Sie war müde (es mochte wohl halb drei Uhr sein), aber sie ließ ihn keinen Mißmut merken. Wortlos legte sie ihm Decken auf ein Feldbett zurecht, das hinter einer spanischen Wand stand.

»Leg dich nieder«, sagte sie, »und gib mir das Kokain.«

Sie wußte, daß sie vergeblich um das Kokain bat und daß sie es ihm auch nicht mit Gewalt würde entreißen können.

Tobias schüttelte den Kopf. Er hatte die Kerze auf einen Stuhl neben das Bett gestellt und hockte auf dem Bettrand, mit stieren Augen die Freundin anglotzend, die sich wieder niederlegte.

»Hast du die Tür gut wieder abgeschlossen? Sind die Fenster zu?« fragte er sie.

»Ja, ja doch!«

Er zog die Jacke aus.

Da seufzte Marion und wandte den Kopf ab.

In der Tat! Er bot einen gräßlichen Anblick!

Beide Hemdsärmel waren bis zum Handgelenk herab steif und schwarz von Blut. Übler Geruch wehte daraus auf.

»Bitte, mach schnell«, flüsterte Marion, »und mach keine Blutflecken in die Laken.«

Sie lag immer noch abgewandt. Übelkeit stieg ihr auf. Plötzlich erhob sie sich und erbrach in die Ecke des Zimmers. Sie weinte vor sich hin.

Tobias, ratlos und verzweifelt, begann laut zu brüllen. Er schüttelte die erhobenen Fäuste über seinem Haupt und blickte mit weit aufgerissenen Augen zur Decke empor.

Marion, totenblaß, lief schnell zu ihm hin und verschloß ihm mit der Hand den Mund.

»Stille, still«, flüsterte sie ihm ins Ohr, »es darf dich niemand hören, sonst fliege ich hier raus!«

Nein! Niemand hörte diesen verzweifelten Menschen, *am wenigsten jener gütige Vater, dessen unerbittliche schwarze*

Stirn vor den großen Atelierfenstern stand, starr, unberührt, unbeweglich!

»Komm, leg dich hin und sei ruhig«, sagte Marion, »ich möchte schlafen. Mach das Licht aus.«

Tobias entkleidete sich vollständig. Marion schaute krampfhaft weg. Auch der untere Rand seines Hemdes war voll Blut von den Injektionsstichen in beide Oberschenkel. Es war sein einziges Hemd, das er seit drei Wochen trug; alle andere Wäsche hielt seine Zimmerwirtin in Charlottenburg zurück, als Pfand für die schuldige Miete. Er stank, sich selbst ein Abscheu, widerlich, verhaßt.

Er stellte die Medizinflasche auf den Stuhl, legte die Spritze zurecht, streckte sich unbedeckt auf das Lager aus und löschte die Kerze.

Atemlos wartete er einige Minuten und starrte regungslos zur Decke empor, die auf dieser Zimmerseite bis zur Hälfte und halb zur Wand herab aus Glas war.

Marion regte sich nicht. Durch das Zimmer schlich, träge, schleimig, die Nachtzeit. Es war, als zögen sich quer durch das Atelier, von einer Wand zur andern hin und her, dunkle klebrige Fäden, die einen Duft von geronnenem Blut ausströmten vermischt mit dem süßlichen Parfüm des Kokains und dem lebhafteren des Äthers.

Es war totenstill. Marion schien zu schlafen. Nur der Nachtwind ließ manchmal die Scheiben der Fenster leise klirren. Tobias mahlte laut mit den Zähnen, wie er immer tat, wenn die Kokainvergiftung in ein bestimmtes Stadium getreten war. Dabei verzerrte sich sein Gesicht, und die Schläfen spielten wie Wellen. War nicht neulich, auf dem Alexanderplatz, eine alte hinkende Frau schreiend vor ihm geflüchtet, als sie dieses fratzenschneidende Gesicht sah?

Das Denken stand ihm still. Er lag regungslos und stierte zur Glasdecke hinauf. Von Zeit zu Zeit gab er sich im Dunkeln und ohne näher hinzusehen Kokaininjektionen. Er fühlte an seinen mißhandelten Oberschenkeln, an den zerfetzten Ober- und Unterarmen das Blut rinnen. Gewiß tropfte es auch in die Bettlaken, die zu schonen Marion ihn gebeten hatte. Er kümmerte sich nicht mehr darum. jetzt war er schon in einem Grade vergiftet, daß er, fast mechanisch, in immer kürzeren Zeitabständen Spritzen nehmen *mußte, wie etwas Selbstverständliches, etwa wie Atmen oder Essen, nur um überhaupt weiterzuexistieren.*

Plötzlich wurde er auf Schatten aufmerksam, die über die Glaswände und das halbe Glasdach des Ateliers hinglitten. Er beobachtete sie eine Zeitlang mißtrauisch.

Wenn er genau hinschaute, glaubte er deutlich zu sehen, daß es die Schatten von Menschen waren, Köpfe, Arme, Beine, die sich da am Rand des Daches zu schaffen machten.

Nun drang auch schon durch das Glas ein leises Geflüster. Tobias unterschied drei Stimmen. Männerstimmen, die eifrig redeten. Argwöhnisch beobachtete er die Schatten. Er sah, wie sie sich Werkzeuge reichten, Hebel, Zangen, Brecheisen, und das Geflüster, die leisen Ausrufe paßten sich genau den Bewegungen an.

»*Achtung!*« hörte er. »*Eins ... zwei ... drei ... – hupp!*« Und dann ein deutliches Knacken.

Ein Wind entstand im Zimmer, ein kalter Hauch, der von oben zu kommen schien. Tobias fühlte ihn mit dem ganzen Körper.

Eine schnell sich steigernde Furcht befiel ihn. Das waren Einbrecher! Oder Detektive! ... Hatte nicht der Maler Ludwig M. ... vom Südwestkorso, nicht weit von hier, von einem Einbrecher erzählt, dem er zwischen den Speichern begegnet war, als er in sein Atelier gehen wollte?

Lähmende Angst brannte ihm die Kehle aus. Er lag hier hilflos, blutend, krank bis auf den Tod. Marion schlief, ein wehrloses Mädchen. Waren es Einbrecher so konnten die kurzen Prozeß mit ihnen machen. Waren es Detektive, so würden sie beide in Schutzhaft genommen werden, und gegen ihn, Tobias, würde man Anklage erheben. Er würde in eine Anstalt kommen, jahrelang, und kein Kokain mehr erhalten.

Leise stand er auf und rüttelte die Freundin wach; sie hatte fest geschlafen.

Erschreckt fuhr sie auf.

»Was ist denn? Was ist?«

Tobias deutete flüsternd zur Glasdecke hinauf: »Siehst du? Siehst du die Leute dort?« lallte er.

Die Schatten bewegten sich immer noch.

»Welche Leute?« fragte Marion ängstlich.

»Dort, dort, die Schatten auf dem Dache«, sagte Tobias, »das sind Einbrecher oder Geheimagenten. Um Gottes willen, was sollen wir tun, Marion?«

Marion, nun ganz wach, schaute Tobias entsetzt in die Augen.

»Unsinn!« sagte sie. »Das sind die Schatten der Bogenlampe von unten, von der Straße.«

Tobias schüttelte den Kopf.

»Bogenlampen werfen keine Schatten«, flüsterte er und stierte verzerrten Angesichts zur Decke hinauf.

Marion begann an seinem Verstand zu zweifeln. – *Ist's schon so weit mit ihm?* dachte sie.

Eine dumpfe Angst kroch ihr das Rückgrat hinauf. Mit diesem Wahnsinnigen, dem sie ausgeliefert war, allein in einem schlafenden Hause! Sie wußte sich keinen Rat. Es galt ihn zu beruhigen. Wenn der Tag kam, würde man weiter sehen. Sie sprach auf ihn ein: »Natürlich doch, das sind die Schatten der Bäume unten und der Schornsteine und Windfänge auf dem Dach. Die Bogenlampe schwingt unten im Wind, und das bewegt die Schatten. Geh schlafen, leg dich nieder!«

Das leuchtete Tobias nicht recht ein, doch beruhigte er sich ein wenig. Er würde wachen und beobachten.

»Wo hast du denn deinen Revolver? Du hast doch einen kleinen Revolver, wo ist er denn?« fragte er.

Sie aber hütete sich, ihm die Waffe zu geben.

»Ich weiß jetzt nicht, wo er liegt«, sagte sie, »leg dich nur, das sind keine Einbrecher.«

Tobias beschloß, wenn Marion schliefe, nach dem Revolver zu suchen. Er legte sich hin und belauerte die Schatten, die stetig hin und her schwankten und sich allerhand zu reichen schienen.

Trüber Schein fiel schon durch die Scheiben, deren Ränder klarer und schärfer wurden. Der erste Streif des Morgens dämmerte auf.

VII

Tobias hielt die Flasche empor gegen das Licht. Entsetzen befiel ihn. Es war nur noch ein ganz geringer Rest der Flüssigkeit darin, kaum einen Finger breit über dem Flaschenboden. Ein unnennbares Grauen klammerte sich in seinen Nacken … Kein Kokain mehr! …

Und der Tag kam herauf, *der verhaßte Tag*, der ihn unter die Menschen treiben würde, *die alle seine Feinde sind und vor denen er sich maßlos fürchtete*. Er wand sich auf dem Lager hin und her, in dumpfer Verzweiflung. Der Kopf erhitzte sich ihm mehr und mehr in dieser Angst; eine Art heißer Wut trieb ihn dazu, noch zwei Injektionen zu nehmen. Den Rest der Flasche trank er aus. – Das Mundinnere war fühllos wie Sammet, wie behaart. Er fuhr mit dem Finger in den Mund, ganz tief, bis in den Schlund.

Nun war die große Not da! Was sollte er nun beginnen? Was war ihm die Zeit, was war ihm das Dasein ohne das Gift, nach welchem sein Körper und seine Seele schrie, nach dem sein ganzes Wesen lechzte?

Vergessen die Furcht vor den Einbrechern oder Detektiven, erloschen die Angst vor dem Irrenhaus! Nur eines erfüllte ihn, nur eines brannte sein Inneres aus: – der unbeugsame, unerbittliche, unwiderstehliche, dieser metaphysischunergründliche Trieb, der Wunsch nach dem Gift, das ihm Atem und Leben, Luft und Trank, Sein und Zeit bedeutete!

Mit fieberischen Händen entzündete er die Kerze. Er wollte ganz genau nachsehen, ob wirklich nichts mehr in der Flasche war. Er hatte sie zwar eben, in dieser Minute noch, ausgetrunken, aber sein Wunsch siegte sinnlos über die Logik, *es konnte, ja es konnte sein,* daß noch ein wenig in der Flasche war! Oder, vielleicht hatte er am Abend *zwei Flaschen* gekauft, ohne bis jetzt daran zu denken? Oder vom letzten Male stand hier im Zimmer irgendwo noch eine verborgen?

Er hielt die Flasche gegen das Kerzenlicht. Nein, nein, nein! Nichts darin! Er stülpte sie um, er reckte tief die Zunge in den Flaschenhals hinein. Nichts darin!

Da war's wie ein ferner Donner, der das Zimmer umfah, und ein Leuchten drang rötlich durch die Fenster. Der Tag quoll mächtig empor und grollte ihm dumpf.

Er stieg vom Bett und suchte, auf den Knien rutschend, sich mit seinem Blut, das in dicken Tropfen auf dem Fußboden vor dem Bette lag, besudelnd, das Zimmer ab. Er traute nicht der Kraft seiner Augen. Er betastete jeden Gegenstand, nahm ihn in die Hand und hielt ihn dicht vor die Augen. Konnte das nicht eine Kokainflasche sein, oder jenes, oder dies? Wer sagte ihm, daß ihn seine Augen nicht trogen? *War das, was wie ein Pantoffel aussah, wirklich ein Pantoffel, nichts anderes? Wer konnte es wissen?*

Ach, soviel er auch suchte, er fand nichts.

Im untersten Fach der Kommode fiel ihm, als er auf dem Bauche hinrutschte, der Revolver in die Hände und eine Anzahl Patronen, die dabeilagen. Er legte beides auf einen Stuhl. Aber die Schatten waren fort.

Lieblich strahlten die Fenster in zartem Rosa, aus dem sich der junge Sommertag erhob, klar und ruhig, in majestätischer Größe. *Hei, da pfiffen die lieben Vöglein wieder und lärmten im Licht.*

VIII

Tobias richtete sich auf und wandte sich dem Fenster zu.

Sprachlos stand er in dem gewaltsamen Licht, das sich im Osten gebar und auf ihn hereinbrach, auf diesen geschändeten, blutig zerfetzten Körper, der sich ihm unbewußt hingab wie einem himmlischen Bade. Tobias öffnete das Fenster und erschauerte unter dem frischen Hauch, der ihn traf.

Marion, der goldene Engel, schlief fest. Tobias ging in das Badezimmer nebenan und ließ warmes Wasser in die Wanne laufen. Er wusch seine Wunden und den ganzen Leib, der hie und da nervös zuckte unter der Berührung seiner Hände. Dann hüllte er sich in sein blutiges Hemd und kleidete sich an. Die kleine Weckuhr zeigte fast sieben Uhr.

Er trat an Marions Bett und schaute lange die Schlafende an. Schließlich beugte er sich nieder und küßte sie auf die Stirn.

Sie erwachte.

»Marion«, sagte er, »ich muß gehen. Hast du ein Stückchen Brot da? Mich hungert.«

»Bleib hier«, sagte sie, »ich werde aufstehen und etwas kochen.«

Er trat zurück, hinter den Wandschirm, und setzte sich auf sein Lager. Große Blutflecken waren im Kopfkissen und in den Laken, die ganz zerknüllt über das Bett und den Fußboden verstreut lagen. Auf dem Stuhl neben dem Bett fand Tobias noch den Revolver. Er lud die sechs Lager der Trommel und steckte den Revolver zu sich.

Er war ganz ruhig geworden und unendlich müde. Marion hatte sich angezogen und war ins Badezimmer gegangen, um die Suppe auf dem Gasofen anzurichten.

Tobias starrte wortlos durchs Fenster in das Brachfeld der Vorstadt hinab.

Hier wurde noch gebaut. Grundstücke, mit Drahtgittern umhegt und mit schmutzigem Gras bewachsen, lagen da. Asphaltierte Straßen, in denen noch keine Häuser standen, kreuzten sich und liefen geruhsam im Glanz der Morgensonne hin. *Vögel sangen mild.* Ein tiefes Blau stand am Himmel und sandte linden Hauch. Schäfchenwolken wanderten langsam im Azur.

Marion brachte die Suppe, die dick und nahrhaft war und ihm wohl mundete. Einige Scheiben trockenen Brotes, die sie ihm gab, aß er dazu. Wie immer, nachdem die magennervenlähmende Wirkung des Giftes aufhörte, regte sich ein mächtiger Hunger und Durst. Er aß zwei Teller der Suppe aus. Marion war freundlich und gut und plauderte mit ihm. Sie bat ihn nicht, vom Kokain zu lassen. Sie wußte, daß es vergebens war.

In ihm war eine große Dankbarkeit für dies milde Geschöpf, das einzige, das ihn nicht verstieß, ihn, den Paria ohne Freunde, den jedes Haus ausspie wie einen eklen Auswurf.

»Hast du Geld?« fragte sie ihn.

Er schüttelte stumm den Kopf.

»Ich habe noch eine Mark, davon kann ich dir fünfzig Pfennige geben. Und hier: Speisemarken für die Volksküche.«

Sie gab es ihm.

Da legte er den Kopf auf den Tischrand und begann zu weinen. Ein tiefes Schluchzen brach aus ihm hervor. Er ergriff die gute Mädchenhand und legte sein irres Antlitz hinein. Tränen netzten sie. Marion strich ihm leise übers Haar: *»Armer Tobias!«*

IX

Eine Zeitlang saß er noch. Dann ergriff er seinen Hut, küßte ihr die Hand und ging.

Im Treppenhaus achtete er darauf, daß ihn niemand sah. Seltsam war es, hier hinabzusteigen, wo die Gespenster ihr Wesen mit ihm getrieben hatten. Er fühlte einen schalen Geschmack im Munde.

Unten, vor der Haustür, begrüßte ihn ein klarer und heiterer Sonnenschein.

Tobias streifte in das Gelände hinaus, ging ziellos durch die leeren Straßen. Nur selten begegnete ihm jemand zu dieser frühen Morgenstunde.

Da begannen die Glocken der umliegenden Kirchen zu schwingen, es war ein beständiges, lang hinhallendes Singen in der Luft, die feiner und durchsichtiger war, als er es je erlebt hatte.

Über schön angelegte Plätze wanderte er und bewunderte die farbigen Häuser, die unbegreiflich ruhig, wie geschliffen, sich zu diesem Himmel voll Gesang erhoben. Es war Sonntag. Wolken, klein und strahlend weiß, segelten langsam hoch im Blauen dahin und sammelten sich im Hafen des Horizonts.

Tobias kam zur Kaiserallee.

Trams klingelten heran und jagten tobend an ihm vorbei, in einem Wirbel von Leben und Bewegung.

Am Friedrich-Wilhelm-Platz strich Tobias um die rote Kirche herum. Er wollte hineingehen. Aber als er sich dem Eingang näherte, spürte er die Gegenwart von Menschen.

Wieder befiel ihn diese düstere Scheu, diese aus Nacht und Qual geborene Angst, die ihn von allen Tischen, von allen Menschen und aus allen Räumen forttrieb.

Nichts blieb ihm!

Er blieb stehen und öffnete die Hand. Er schaute seine Hand an, lange und wie in tiefem Sinnen. Dann betrachtete er seinen schmierigen Anzug, die schadhaften Stiefel. Durch die Ärmel des hellen Jacketts drangen Blutflecke, auch die Hose zeigte Spuren.

Als Schritte hinter ihm ertönten, fuhr er zusammen.

Es war der Priester, der zur Kirche ging.

Tobias ging langsam weiter, an den Vorgärten der Allee entlangschlendernd.

Da saßen auf den kleinen Balkonen Vater, Mutter und Kinder und frühstückten. *Heiteres Lachen erklang.* Tobias starrte verstohlen hin. Hunger regte sich neu.

… *Da wußte er, daß er den Abend dieses Sonntags nicht erleben würde.*

Nicht mehr würde ihn der mächtige Dämon ergreifen und ihn in die Düsternis stoßen.

Er hatte nichts, daran er sich erfreuen konnte. Besitzlos, verstoßen, krank und verflucht war er. Kein Essen, kein Geld, keine Kleidung, keine Wohnung, keinen Freund und keinen Mitmenschen hatte er. Und nicht den Willen, nicht die Kraft, es zu erwerben.

Das Gift nur, das sein Schicksal war, lagerte wie ein riesiges Tier über der ganzen Stadt, über den Horizonten und über seinem, Dasein: – unentrinnbar, *Charybdis, die ihn schlürfte.*

Ausgefetzt würde er sich hinstehlen sein Leben lang, vom Morgen bis zum Abend, der ihm einst den Wahnsinn bringen würde.

Er trat in einen Hausflur und zog den Revolver hervor. Er entsicherte ihn und überlegte den besten Schuß. Schließlich öffnete er den Mund und preßte die Mündung der Waffe an den Gaumen. *So war es gut.*

Er drückte ab. Dröhnend hallte der Schuß durchs Haus. Tobias stürzte zusammen wie in einem Kniefall.

Herbeigeeilte Hausbewohner fanden ihn tot. Teile seines Gehirns hingen überall, an den Wänden, am Geländer und auf den Stufen der Treppe.

Draußen pfiffen die Vöglein, und eine Straßenbahn lärmte durch den Morgen hin, die Allee hinab, nach Berlin zu.

DIE ERNIEDRIGUNG
– EIN TOTENTANZ

I

Wer ist mehr berufen, die Mächte über sich zu fühlen, als der Dichter? Wer mehr berufen, alle Schauerlichkeit ihrer hallenden Grotten auszutrinken, als er, der Berufene *kat' exochän*, der Bejaher, der ewig Kämpfende am Ölberge, der da spricht: »Ist es nicht möglich, daß dieser Kelch von mir gehe, ich trinke ihn denn; so geschehe dein Wille! ...« Er lebt auf allen Inseln; er stürzt in jede Stadt; erfrorner Sperling, schwebt auf jeden Park hernieder; und jede Nacht ist ihm feindlich! – Nur wer dienet, mag befehlen! ... So dient er, der Prinz, und über Nacht und Finsternis wird er König, triumphaler Rufer und Herrscher des Lichts. – So fiel er in (trostlose) Wüste orientalischen Giftes: er, der Berufene, Tobias Sternraffer, der Dichter. –

Ein Uhr durch! ... Voll Grauen schritt er über die Schiffsbrücke. Die Pontons ächzten, quatschige Wasser-Tiere, unter seinem eiligen Schritt. Der Dom, ein aufgeschreckter Riesen-Hase, floh mit langen Ohren in trübe Ferne. Ein Dampfer hastete verloren, mit plätschernden Rädern, in die Finsternis. Licht-Blut einer Fabrik am Ufer pulste durch Stangen-Geripp und schmierige Fenster-Augen. Seine Hand in der Ulstertasche umschmeichelte die Medizinflasche. Ein tiefes Grauen vorn im Hirn, an der Peripherie des Schädels, im Auge, im Nacken; und ein makabrer Drang, ein unergründliches, unbegreifliches unwiderstehliches Sehnen nach dem Gift im Rückgrat: – so saß er, verkrochen, in der Trambahn. Nicht konnte er es erwarten, nach Hause zu kommen.

Mutter und Schwester schliefen schon. Aber die Katze leuchtete in seinem Zimmer. Er entzündete das Gas und legte auf dem Bett-Stuhl Flasche, Spritze, Watte, Tuch und Kerze zurecht. Kaum den Überrock abgeworfen, gab er sich zwei starke Spritzen (Sol. hydro. Cocaine 0,06) in den Oberarm. Seine Füße hoben sich vom Boden, das Haar schäumte, er schwebte an der Zimmerdecke und trank den Glanz des Gaslichts. Eifrigst entkleidete er sich.

Noch war er nicht zu Bett, so fühlte er schon das dunkle Tuch von oben auf sich herniederschweben, das ihn fest einwickelte, Mund, Nase, Ohr und Lunge dick verhüllend und ihn in eine Ecke drückte. Dort schrumpfte er ganz klein zusammen. Die Augen rissen sich auf; die Pupillen weiteten sich zu zwei unabsehbaren schwarzen Schächten … Ah!, den Druck vom Körper fort! – Hastig nahm er zwei weitere Spritzen. Sofort ward ihm wohler und unendlich ruhig. Die Augen schlossen sich. Doch dann gingen sie wieder wie zwei dunkle Monde auf: weit! weit! … Die Hand zitterte ein wenig. Er floh ins Bett. – Die Möbel begannen zu flüstern, und die Fenster-Vorhänge machten eine leise Musik. Das Zimmer schwankte, ein langsam sinkendes Schiff. Halt! man könnte ihn beobachten! … Er verhüllte sorgfältig die Fenster, schloß die Zimmertür ab und hing seinen Hut an die Klinke. – Doch die Photographien auf der Kommode konnten den geheimen Beobachtern vielleicht als Spiegel dienen! Er legte sie platt nieder, nahm selbst einen Spiegel zur Hand und belauerte angestrengtest die Vorgänge in dem Teil des Zimmers, dem er den Rücken zuwenden mußte.

Die Angst wuchs … Die Tapeten belebten sich mit Augen, die langsam auf und nieder kreisten und strenge blickten. Er schreckte auf und sah sich um. Doch sofort warf er den Körper wieder zurück, denn unter dem Sofa bewegte sich etwas … Sollte es seine Schwester sein, die der schlafenden Mutter Lichtsignale gab über seinen Zustand und die Anzahl der Spritzen? … Er sprang auf, suchte unter dem Sofa, nahm eine neue Spritze, lachte (es war die Katze), löschte das Gaslicht und legte sich von neuem zu Bett.

Mit großen Augen lag er da. Die Katze schlich leise im Zimmer umher. – Neue Angst erfaßte ihn. Er hörte deutlich Stimmen, die Stimmen seiner Mutter und seiner Schwester. Schnell nahm er eine Spritze. Nun schwieg es ein wenig. Doch plötzlich klingelte es (mitten in der Nacht!), die Tür ging, jemand trat nebenan ins Zimmer. In seinem Handspiegel konnte Tobias nun auf irgend eine Weise (über die er nicht weiter nachdachte) das Zimmer nebenan sehen. – Dort brannte Licht. Mutter und Schwester saßen, im Nachtgewand, am Tisch; der Hereingetretene war Dr. Pagenstecher, der Apotheker, von dem er das Kokain bezog. Er hatte den Hut in der Hand und den Überzieher an und schüttelte langsam und mitleidig den Kopf. Die Mutter weinte. Jetzt hörte Tobias ganz deutlich die Schwester sprechen: »Ist das nicht fürchterlich mit Tobias? … Wie er die Augen aufreißt! Man sollte einen Arzt holen! Er wird wahnsinnig!« Der Apotheker nickte traurig. Die Mutter schluchzte: »Ja, Herr Pagenstecher, holen Sie den Arzt!« Der Apotheker wandte sich und ging. Die Mutter hatte, in tiefem Gram, den Kopf in die Hände auf den Tisch gelegt.

II

O Gott! der Arzt! ... – Tobias fuhr auf und versuchte mit fieberhaften Händen die Kerze zu entzünden. Erst das sechste Streichholz fing Feuer. Er nahm eine Spritze. Inzwischen drang der Tag, grau und langsam, schleichend, durch das vermummte Fenster. Tobias, über die Katze stolpernd, die aufrecht saß, in beiden Vorderpfoten kleine Spiegel hielt und Lichtsignale gab, schloß, erst leise, dann mit einem Ruck, seine Zimmertür auf und glotzte bohrend in den Korridor hinein. Im Hintergrund stand dort eine alte Truhe, und Tobias sah auf ihr deutlich die Gestalt seiner Mutter sitzen, die das kummerzerfressene Antlitz zu verbergen trachtete und heimlich nach ihm schaute. Die Schwester, Ly, hatte sich hinter den Kleidern am Garderobenständer verborgen und schnalzte mißbilligend mit der Zunge. Tobias starrte lange hin. Schließlich sagte er stockend (und die Stimme klebte ihm schlaff und fetzenweise am Gaumen) in den Flur hinaus: »Mutter! ... laß das doch! ... Ich seh dich ja! ... Ich habe nur eine einzige Spritze genommen!« Das Blut stieg ihm kalt zu Kopfe vor dieser Lüge, aber er hielt sie für notwendig, um die Mutter zu beruhigen, der große Tränen aus den Augen flossen. Sie regte sich nicht. »Na, ich ... ich ... ich sehs ja doch! ...« sagte Tobias. Wie er sich umwandte, sah er die Schwester ins Zimmer huschen, wie sie gerade hinter der Gardine am Fenster verschwand. Er schloß wieder ab.

Zagend schlich er auf die Gardine zu; aber noch ehe er sie erreicht hatte, war Ly durch das geschlossene Fenster hinausgesprungen. Er sah nach, ob sie sich vielleicht noch am Fensterbrett festhalte. Aber sie lag zerschmettert unten auf der Straße und bewegte den qualvollen Leib.

Menschen sammelten sich langsam an. – Tobias zitterte an allen Gliedern. Er setzte sich aufs Bett und gab sich zwei Injektionen hintereinander. Bei der zweiten hatte er die Nadel zu tief eingestochen; flink quoll ein dünnes, hellrotes Rinnsal, kroch vom Oberarm bis zum Handgelenk, tropfte auf den Schenkel und lief das Bein entlang bis zur Fußsohle. Es sah aus wie Eisenbahnlinien auf einer Landkarte. Die Watte tränkte sich rot, so oft Tobias das Blut zu stillen versuchte. Höhnisches Gerinn! Schließlich schien ihm, als ob er aus tausend Stichen und aus allen Körperöffnungen blute. Todesangst packte ihn. Er ließ den Strömen ihren Lauf. Jetzt ward es heller Tag. Eine gläserne Sonne sandte kalte Blendstrahlen auf die umliegenden hohen fünfstöckigen Häuser; die riesigen Dächer schienen zu flattern, und auf die Straße fielen die Sonnenstrahlen wie Millionen Nadeln. Tobias schleppte sich ans Fenster, um nach der Schwester zu sehen. – Auf der Straße war es schwarz von Menschen, einer stoßenden, drängenden Menge, die schweigend und starr zu Tobias hinaufblickte, mit schadenfrohen und bösen Gesichtern.

Tobias suchte krampfhaft auf dem Fußboden herum. Was suchte er doch? … Nadeln, die Schwester, oder einen Teil des anmutigen, zerschmetterten Körperchens? Seine Hände und Knie waren voll Schmutz, denn die müde Mutter reinigte längst nicht mehr Tobias' Zimmer. Unzählige Streichhölzer, Watte, Kerzen- und Blutstropfen lagen herum. Tobias nahm alles in die Finger, nestelte daran und betrachtete es

118 | WALTER RHEINER

genauest. Er hatte Angst, alle diese Gegenstände könnten die Schwester sein, und er sähe nur so falsch … Er kam wieder dem Fenster nahe. Drunten staute sich die Menge, blickte aufmerksam herauf und befragte sich gegenseitig, murmelnd. Aber auch auf den Dächern der gegenüberliegenden Häuser, in allen Fenstern, auf allen Balkonen wimmelte es von Leuten, Männern und Frauen, zum Teil mit Fernrohren und Operngläsern, alle aber einzig seinethalben aufgestellt und ihm zuschauend. Mutter und Schwester, im Nachtkleid, frierend, waren darunter. Iris, die Katze, spazierte hämisch, mit ironischen Pfoten, über die tausend Köpfe hin. Dr. Pagenstecher, der Apotheker, stand auf dem mittleren Balkon und erklärte, mit den Armen deutend, einer Schar Polizisten Tobias Sternraffers schlimmen Fall. Die hörten zu; Helme und Gummiknüppel nickten. Tobias verstand zwar kein Wort, doch war es keine Frage, daß man über ihn sprach, über ihn!

Jetzt wandten sich plötzlich alle Polizisten um und schauten scharf nach Tobias; einer trat vor (die Menschenmenge rauschte, ein Meer) und (es war der Polizeihauptmann in glitzernder Uniform) schrie herüber:

»He! Sie! Sie da! Zum Donnerwetter! Lassen Sie das jetzt sein! Schämen Sie sich nicht!? Sie Tier!!« Beifall, Händeklatschen bei dem Volk unten. Immer neue kamen aus nahen Straßenzügen, die Balkone füllten sich mehr und mehr und ein tosendes, langhinhallendes Geschrei hub an: »He! Sie da! He! Herr Sternraffer! Herr Sternraffer! … Schluß! Schluß! Aufhören! He! Herr Sternraffer!«

Einige sprangen von den Balkonen herunter und kletterten eilig an der Fassade des Hauses empor, auf Tobias' Zimmerfenster zu. Der lallte, in Schweiß gebadet:

»Nun … nun … Aber … aber … das Haus … bricht ja
…« Ja, es brach. – Zuerst wankte der hohe Schrank, satanisch
grinsend. Das Bett knickte bäuchlings ein. Ein Tosen
schwoll, ein Gedröhn!; violette Sonnen tanzten. Schrank und
Möbel neigten sich langsam und weit vor! Tobias versuchte
zu schreien; der Laut blieb ihm stecken. Im Stürzen sah er
noch, wie drüben alle Balkone abbröckelten und mit den
Zuschauern pfeifend in die Tiefe fuhren … Im Ozean von
Getöse und Licht versank alles …

III – REQUIEM

Der Apotheker aber (… seht ihrs denn nicht? …) ist
CHRISTUS JESUS, der über den zerfallenen Häusern und
über den verfallenen Menschen sitzet und mitleidig den Kopf
schüttelt. Er hat den Hut in der Hand und wird den Arzt holen.
Aus seiner Ulstertasche zieht er eine große Mond-Harfe. Er
weint, und wie die Tränen auf die Saiten fallen, erklingt es
leise: Du Menschensohn! Nicht spendet der Himmel Blick
und gutes Wort zu tödlichem Jammertanz. Ein Marter-
Regen, dumpfe Tränen, kränzen (o Bitternis!) eure Häupter.
Ihr arm Gebein! Verkrochen in Not und Tod, entzündet Gott
des mühsamen Hirnes Schrein … Du Mensch bist groß! und
Dornen-Krone trägst du, und Kreuzigung tausendfache! …
… Und Tobias Sternraffer, der ihn sieht, Tobias, zerweinten
Körpers der Mutter armes Haupt im Schoß, schreit! schreit!:
seid gut! seid gut!!

DREI FRAGMENTE AUS EINER KRIEGSNOVELLE

I

Am Abend brodelten ihre Köpfe, irre Kugeln, in der Dorfschenke. Der Regen peitschte an die schmalen Fensterscheiben. Oft klang es wie fernes Hufgetrappel einer großen Reiterschar, die ununterbrochen das Dorf umritt, einzelne Scharen vorwarf, andere zurückzog. Der Geruch des Regens drang durch die Holzwände und durchtränkte die Dunst-Schwaden der Zigaretten und des Tabaks, die über die wirren Angesichter wanderten. Zwei trübe Lampen quollen und kreisten langsam an der Decke, die bald nahe schien, bald fern. Ein langsamer Rhythmus bewegte die Glieder der Soldaten, die puppenhaft, abgestorben auf den Tischen und Bänken umherlagen und lang über den Boden schlurften. In der Ecke ein schlechtes Klavier, eine falsche Geige, deren Töne wie Drähte durchs Zimmer schwirrten, in zackigen Takten. Des Geigers stieres Auge blinkte über der Violine; er grinste teuflisch, wenn er sah, wie die Töne die enggedrängte Schar maskenhaft bewegten. Köpfe und Schultern wogten hin und her, taumelnd. Nicht erkannte einer den andern. »Kamerad«, »Bier«, »Gib Feuer«, »Die Russen«, »Bauch-schuß«, schrie es. Die Billardkugeln knallten. Einer hatte Streit, war zornig; sein Gesicht, blutrot, sah wie gespalten aus: ein Axthieb lief bis zur hochgezogenen Oberlippe. Olaf hockte eng in einer Ecke. Verfaultes zersetzte sich in ihm, eine fahle Flamme schwelte in seinem Innern. Ein Walzer taumelte aus der Musik-Ecke auf. (»*Les baisers sont flétris*«, singt es in Olaf mit.) Ein Akrobat tanzte ihn auf den Händen. Berlin war weit, die große glühende Spinne. Es rollte davon, weit weg, überschlug sich, zog alle Städte an seinen Fäden nach. Der Wind stürmte ums Haus, die Musik, das Gespräch knarrte. Alle Gesichter waren blank, teigig aufgegangen. *Man wußte: draußen wimmeln die Millionen.* Die große Schlange im Osten und Westen windet sich unaufhörlich. Sie dreht sich um sich selbst, speit Gift. Ein Hochwald von Kanonen starrt in die Wolken. Breite Flüsse von Blut fließen ins Meer; Leicheninseln zerfallen. Hier aber hocken neue Massen Fleisch. Weiß und kalt ist der Qualm des Tabaks. Ermattung senkt sich. Man schweigt, zwei, drei Sekunden, in denen süß und leise die Bilder geliebter Frauen aus den Augen treten, die sie innen schauten. Dann wieder Lärm. Erids Antlitz zitterte groß und deutlich an der Decke. Ein Dunststreif machte die Bewegung ihrer Schulter. Olaf versank. Man kroch ins feuchte Stroh. Einzelne Sterne kamen, dann wieder Regen. Nasse Mäuse über die heißen Lippen. Eine ferne Trompete, langsames Signal. Man stierte ins Dunkel. Schlief endlich ein, im grauenden Morgen, fröstelnd.

II

Ein krachendes Gewölbe, schließt die Nacht ihren schwarzen Ring um die Heere. Feurige Bänder schlingen sich über den Scheiteln der Geduckten. Schnüren den Atem der Tausende fester. Große Garben von Heu- und Leichenduft wandern über die Fluren. Versteckte kleine Feuer schwelen atemlos und ängstlich, von schmalen Antlitzen schattenhaft umstellt. Rauh lallen Befehle, schleichen sich an den Erdwänden der Schützengräben weiter. Man flüstert, schweigt. Der Himmel aber tobt; Schollen treiben darin; er bröckelt, bricht. Stürzen nicht riesige schwarze Schalen herab, in denen, eingeschüchtert, kleine Sterne schwimmen? Das Feld vor den Gräben ist ein brodelnder heißer See. Erdwellen kochen, Hügel-Blasen platzen. Es wogt. Wie Geysire steigen die Granaten auf. Aus dem Bauch der Erde scheinen sie zu kommen. Plötzlich schlagen die Granaten im regelmäßigen Rhythmus auf. *Danse macabre!* Schrapnells sprühen auseinander; alle Augen glotzen hinauf. Wozu plötzlich die Vision der Erinnerung: Feuerwerk in der Werkbundausstellung in Köln am Rhein. Feuergüsse von der Rheinbrücke. Glänzende Terrassen, Fontänen, blumige Frauen, Gold und die irisierenden, wollüstig den Atem verhaltenden Takte des *Tango argentino?* Ah! Huschen Wolken über das nächtige Firmament? Fliehen zum Meer? Die Nacht brüllt. Sie birst. Die Nacht ist ein klirrender Metalldeckel, der sich über den Horizont geschoben hat. Nun splittert er, und die Sonne dahinter jubelt in rasendem Feuer. Versunkene Gesichter, lauernd über den Gewehrkolben gebeugt, grell vom Feuer bespien, ohne Ausdruck, maskenhaft. Das Blut zuckt durch den Körper. In einer Sekunde dreimal durch Auge, Herz, Beine,

Hirn; es klopft. *Es will heraus.* Da, eine irre Stimme, sich überschlagend, durch das Dickicht dieses Schweigens: »*Sturm auf! Marsch – marsch!*« Aus den Gräben flackern sie auf, diese verschütteten Flammengesichter; die Glieder zucken empor. Die Arme wirbeln wie Maschinenkolben. Olaf fühlt plötzlich den ganzen Mechanismus seines Körpers. Die Muskeln straffen sich, die Augen liegen fühlbar in den Höhlen; er fühlt die Haare wachsen, fühlt das Spiel der Sehnen in Armen, Beinen, Händen. Die Waffe ist in der Hand. Vorwärts. Die Raubtiere springen. Sie röhren. Speichel fließt aus Mund, Rotz aus Nase, Wasser aus Augen, Poren, Penis. Und das Gehirn liegt auf einer Scheibe, ja, auf einer gläsernen Scheibe, die sich rasend dreht. Es spritzt aus, nach Nord, Süd, voran, rückwärts. Zentrifugalkraft. Der Körper tobt. Ja: Blut auch, *Blut muß auch spritzen!* Und: links liegt das Nordmeer, Ostsee, Weißes Meer; rechts Schwarzes Meer. Sie stehn auf, die Meere, haushoch. Sie brechen ein ins Land. Auf langen Taifunbeinen stelzen sie herein. Und der Himmel nähert sich. Er schüttert von riesigen dunklen Sonnen aus schwarzem Marmor. Und die Wälder biegen sich. Die Sterne baumeln in ihren Ästen. Und dort ist der Feind, die Russen. *Ah! Moskau, Glocken, Schnee!* »Hunde! Freunde! Menschen! Tiere! *Wir Mörder! Ihr Mörder!* Moskau! Berlin!« – »Prußki schtoi!« – »Schtoi, schtoi!« – »Hurrah, urra!« – »Heh!« – »Halt!« – »Aas!« Bajonett in den Wanst! Olaf stößt, rennt nieder, stößt, schießt mit dem Revolver. Ein Schlag gegen seine Schulter. Eine Granate zerreißt eine Gruppe Kameraden. Einer fällt ihm in die Arme, sein Halsstumpf gurgelt ihm heißes Blut ins Gesicht. Rückgrat und Hirn wird eisig, starr. Der Lärm klingt dick und fern. Ah! Das Meer glättet sich! Er sinkt um.

III

Tausend Fahnen stürmen in seiner Seele. Die Trikolore flammt ihm aus den Augen. »Ah! Midinette, ich werde dich niederreiten!« Auf dem Treppenflur huschen, staubig glitzernd im Dämmer, die Gespenster jener grünen und blauen Nächte, die ineinander verkrallten Stunden romantischer Seelenfusion. Ah! Aber die Fronten stehn auf im Osten und Westen, sonnenbeglänzte Städte knattern, und ein neuer Tag stürzt aus den Zügen Tausender, deren Schritte durch die Mittag-Straßen Berlins trommeln. O strahlende Flotte auf den gläsernen Meeren! Arbeit kracht, wühlt, schäumt ringsum. Und der Tag liegt offen und spiegelt den ausgehöhlten blauen Himmel. Schon steht er im Zimmer, und sie weht ihn kühl an, im grünen Schleier, und ihr Haar liegt wieder unerträglich glatt, süchtig, und das Weiße ihrer Augen ist gebogner Mond über Traumteichen. Fort der Traum! Strahlendes Erfassen des wilden, nackten, tanzenden Tags! Und seine neue Stimme, blank und ohne Hülle aufsteigend: »Liebst du mich, Erid?« – »Ich liebe dich, ich war bei dir alle Tage, ich hab mich über dich hinausgeworfen, Ole.« Doch er, hart: »Ich liebe dich, heute. Wenn du mich liebst, so verlaß deinen Mann, geh mit mir. *Ich lebe im Keller, wo Sonne köstlicher Sonntag ist. Scheuche mir nachts die Ratten von der Stirn. Wir werden aus einer Schüssel essen, mit einem Löffel, abwechselnd. Komm!«* Sie zittert. »Ole!« – »Komm, meine Braut, meine Geliebte, gefunden durch die Äonen!« – »Ist dies dein Ernst, Ole? Du weißt, ich kann nicht von ihm gehen. Er …« Und Olaf, unterbrechend: »Ja. Er macht dir das Leben angenehm. Du darfst träumen, singen, schlafen. Nur eins kannst du nicht, arme Frau: lieben. *Bist eine Frau und kannst nicht lieben!*

Komm! Bei mir kannst du lieben. Hilf mir hungern, arbeiten, kämpfen. Wir werden das Leben bezwingen, und die Tat wird blühen, *die selige Tat …*« – Sie schreit auf, laut: »Ole! Sind das deine Worte? Ich kann nicht lieben? Und liebe dich, so tief, so innen, so über allem! Sprich nicht so! Ist das nicht Liebe, tausendmal gefühlt, tausendmal genannt von dir!« – »Nein, Erid, nicht Liebe. *Nur deren Gespenst!* Sieh, wie die Städte gegen den Himmel schwirren! *Arbeit ist, Tat ist!* Nicht Traum. Schwingendes Außen aus herrlichem Innen. Nichts verkriecht in sich (… ah, diese *imitatio coitus* der Seele, denkt er dabei …). Brausendes Oben aus schweigender Tiefe. Und seliges In-Allem statt Über-Allem. Arme! Komm, *ich werde dich das Leben lehren und die große Liebe* (… Blondes Mondschäfchen, lacht sein Herz dazu …). Ganz mein, ganz der Welt, ganz dem Tag. Hei, wie rein die Luft geht, die Berge leuchten und die Flüsse flattern. Und die Kranen klirren. Perlende Schiffe. Und die Sonne schwirrt, jauchzender Diskus! Komm!« – »Ich kann nicht, ich … Ole … bist du Ole?« – »Neu bin ich. Komm, wir schlingen das Band. Wir fahren nach Paris, nach London, nach St. Petersburg, nach Rom, nach New York, den brüderlichen Städten!« Und sie singend: »Nicht kenne ich dich mehr, Olaf, mein Geliebter. Sieh, ich sitze in der Laube, und der Mond wirft singende Netze. Und meine Seele ist bei dir über den Dächern der großen Stadt. Hohe Kantilene dein Schritt, Olaf, mein Du, mein draußen wanderndes Herz. Sieh, wie die Nacht ausblüht aus meinen Augen. Ah, sie trinken den Himmel aus, dich zu treffen. Und dein letzter Handkuß ist ein langsamer Tanz auf diesem Schnee der Hand, Olaf. Wir schlafen ein zu gleicher Zeit, unsere Seele schläft ein. Wo liegen unsere Körper, getrennt oder nah oder weit? Wie sind wir verflochten, und die Welt ist eine perlende Spieluhr in unserer Brust, um die nächtliche Winde wehen ...« Sie schrickt auf, das Gesicht überhell; es fällt, ein Mondstein, vom Himmel.

DER TOD DES SCHWÄRMERS GAUTIER FÉMIN

(EIN ABSCHIED UND EINE BEGRÜSSUNG)

I

Ich will nicht behaupten, daß mein Freund Gautier Fémin, Bureaubeamter im Hause Dreyfus & Cie. in Paris, von jeher romantischer Schwärmer gewesen sei. Zu der Zeit aber, von der ich spreche, war sein Fehler der, daß er zu leicht und ausschließlich an »das Schöne« glaubte: ein Begriff, oder (wie er mich stets verbesserte) ein Erlebnis, mit dem er keineswegs irgendwelche ethischen oder auch nur praktischen Ziele verband. Ästhet also, betonte er des öfteren, daß das Schöne einzig um seiner selbst willen dasei, fremd jeder Tendenz, abgekehrt allem realen Betrieb, wenngleich mitten in ihm (einem aus Schutt und Schmutz ausgegrabenen Torso gleich) vollendet, manifestiert. – Dies war sein zweiter Irrtum und, wie er mir (in der Stunde der Erkenntnis noch in unfreie Mystik verwirrt) kurz vor dem Ereignis sagte, die innere Ursache seines notwendigen Todes.

Es ist möglich, daß seine damalige namenlos Geliebte in der Stunde seiner vollkommenen Abkehr von ihr zu der unschuldigen Kugel wurde, die seinen Selbsttod vollzog. – Dem Studium der Musik zuliebe aus Kristiania nach Paris verpflanzt, hatte Erid ihn im Salon eines jungen Komponisten kennengelernt: – ihn in die Knie Geworfenen vor der mitternachtsonnenhaften Fjord-Landschaft ihres Hauptes und der kühlen Fremdheit ihres Körpers. Nicht lange darauf sah man diese Frau, unter verschwenderischer Ignorierung ihres Gatten wie ihres bisherigen Freundes, Arm in Arm mit ihm durch die farbigen Felder abendlicher Boulevards wallen, schäumen in den Licht-Kaskaden der Konzertsäle und Theater, verschwimmen im rosa Schein und Parfüm der Ateliers efreundeter junger Maler. Oft saßen wir anderen, brennender Gespräche voll, beisammen oder ergingen uns im Abend der Seine-Ufer, und er fehlte, Gautier Fémin, der Schwärmer. Später erfuhr ich von ihm, daß er an solchen Tagen, in klingendem Schweigen oder in leichten Gesprächen (deren Worte aber, golden und tief, wie in einer Tropfstein-Höhle nach innen fielen in aller Stille) mehr und mehr mit Erid verschmolz. Es gab Worte zwischen ihnen und kleine Handlungen, aus denen plötzlich ein Blick erblühte, der ihn ihres tiefsten Wesens Gemeinsamkeit erkennen ließ. Und in langen Spaziergängen, während sie süß und neu die Ebenen der Waldsäume, der Teiche und naher Firmamente im Bois de Boulogne über sich rinnen fühlten, schuf er ihr gemeinsames evangelisches Wort »Du-Dasein«, worin sie sich vollendeten. Hingeraffter Schöpfer maßlosen Idealismus', wandelnd mit allen Schauern Geistes und Körpers unter gemeinsamen Rundgewölben verinnerlichter Tage, erkannte Gautier nicht mehr Sinn und Zweck der nüchternen Zahlen des Kontokorrents,

des vielsprachigen Textes ozeanischer Geschäftsbriefe, der
kargen Befehle des Managers im Bureau von Dreyfus &
Cie. Nach wiederholten Fällen schlechtentschuldigten
Fernbleibens von seiner Arbeit, nach erster mystischer Fahrt
im Bette der Geliebten (... Weltenfahrzeug im unendlichen
gesichteerfüllten Raum! ...) verschlafen und verklärt am Pult
hockend, fand er sich am Abend singenden Mai-Endes, leise
erschrocken, doch rasch besänftigt, an den Häusern der Rue
de la Banque zu den großen Boulevards hintreibend: entlassen,
letztes Gehalt in der Tasche.

II

Von nun an wohnte er, unbekümmert um Hunger und
Geldmangel, bei Coret im dekadenten Atelier, bei Lebref dem
Studenten, bei mir: – grenzenlos ausgegossen in Nichtstun,
Liebe, Spaziergänge, Musik, Cafés und Mond-Nächte mit
Erid. In Haschisch- und Kokain-Räuschen (die ihm Kellner
auf Montmartre gegen gutes Trinkgeld verschafften) träumte
er bald fabelhafteste Seelen-Fusion mit ihr, ekstatisch
verflochtene Zukunft, aufgerichtete Säule, eiffelturmgleich,
vollendeter Einheit, Schönheit zweier Wesen; – bald
wieder befielen ihn Zweifel am soeben proklamierten Ideal,
Experimentier-Projekte nervösester Überspannung, angstvolle
Selbst-Analysen und -Messungen an dem selbsterbauten
unmenschlich-ungeheuren Maßstab. Nicht interessierten
ihn unsere, seiner Freunde, allerirdischste real-soziale und
politische Erörterungen der Kunst. Wohl aber brachte er uns
(wie vorher nie) den Wortlaut seiner hastenden, drängenden,
wirren, ja verzweifelten Gespräche dieser Tage mit Erid. Sie,
aufgestellt, Marmorbild ihm entkörpert fast, fremder Tag

um Tag: – nicht mehr wollte sie seine Angst verstehen, sein Drängen auf Verwirklichung des in Kulmination romantisch-mystischer Ekstase erlebten Gefühls »Du-Dasein«. In Netze norwegischer Lieder einsamst verstrickt, hinschleichend mit dem dekadenten Maler Coret, mit Lebref dem Studenten, zu neuen um Teich-Ufer lügnerisch gewobenen Ekstasen; oft auch daheim nest-täubchenhaft mit ihrem Gatten (dem in Ehren wiedergefundenen) angenehm und sanft Tee schlürfend; ja oft erheitert und mütterlich lächelnd über Gautiers eifrige Qual, doch auch oft prinzlich erzürnt über plötzliche manchmal noch ungewollte Zerstörung kümmerlicher Illusions-Reste durch sein schärfer und härter, nackter, explosiver fallendes Wort: – so ward er ihr gleichgültig erst, unbequem, störend, feindlich zuletzt. Und er, Gautier: allein sitzend oder (selten) fremdartig, verloren und verstört unter uns, mit einer fast anklagenden Stimme mühsamen Spottes von seinem letzten Zusammensein mit Erid erzählend, brachte schon hier und da Worte auf, wie: Zerbinetta-Ariadne! Narzissa! Psycho-Prostitution!, oder: sie geht auf den »inneren« Strich! sie ist schon wieder mit jemand »du-da«! die Fusion ist an ihrem Seelenklappenfehler gescheitert! ... – Er gab die Person auf, glaubte aber noch an die Sache. Und das noch dieser Person bei sich insgeheim wieder abbittend, sie grüßend auf der Straße, gelegentlich noch mit ihr sprechend. – Dann wieder dumpf, kokaingesättigt, versunken, unberührt von anderem: – selbst von plötzlich nahenden Wirbeln politischer Komplikationen, die uns andere hinrissen in erfüllte Abende, treibende Menschenflüsse auf den Boulevards Montmartre und Poissonnière, illuminierte Telegramme, Abfahrt der Ausländer am Ost- und Nordbahnhof, plötzlich auf die Straßenzüge niederstürmende Trikoloren, nächtliche Fackel-

Demonstrationen im Blitz des Eiffelturms, Massenreden und -gesang in den rotbestrahlten Himmel.

III

Tagsüber: Place de la Concorde, aufkreiselnd, bohrend in den blauen unendlich hohen Himmel! Wiesen und Teiche wallten blumig empor, spiegelten Seele und Stern: – vollendeter Sommer! – – – Dann wurde der Krieg erklärt. – Hektisch plötzlich am Horizont lagernde Wolken-Landschaften, seltsam fremd-irres Sausen in Laternen und Bäumen die Boulevards entlang, verworren um Ecken wehende schüttere Antlitze gaben uns Ahnung vielfach überkreuzter wirrer Flächen Blutes, von geborstenen Hügeln herabwandelnd; Ahnung unermeßlichen Scheines jähe aufflatternder Schiffe (… schreiende Fanfaren über den Ozean …); Ahnung nie erschauter Auren furchtbar aufsteigend an Wäldern und Höhen, dröhnender Symphonien in gespenstisch sich ducken den nächtigen Gebirgs-Pässen (… zuckende Leucht-Strahlen verschmelzend in Blut und Feuer zu – endlich! endlich! – tief geahnter neuer Monstranz, sengendem Stirnreif Europas voll schon erwählter herrlicherer Bruderschaft! …) – Vor kurzem noch höchst unwahrscheinliche Kralle sterbend geglaubten Militarismus' (Moloch nun mit schwellendem, alles fressendem Bauch) erfaßte auch uns alle: Coret den dekadenten Maler, Lebref den Studenten, Gautier Fémin und mich … Und unter den Bogen winselnder Granaten, Hammer-Wirbel krampfgeschüttelter Geschütze im Rücken, überschrägt an beiden Flanken von Trommel-Hufen vorstürmender englischer Kavallerie (… »en avant! en avant!« …) geschah es, daß Gautier Fémin, fremden verwehten Antlitzes, mir zu knirschte: »En avant! En avant! – Ihr habt tausendmal echt! – Ich bin nichts

für diese Erde! – Notwendig mein Tod! – Machen wir Schluß!«
– Und während wir einbrachen in die graue Phalanx unserer
Feinde, Blitz der Zukunft vereinzelt aufblitzen sehend an
unseren wie ihren Stirnen, ein schlug in seine die (halluziniert
norwegische) Kugel. Seine willentlich exponierte Silhouette,
aufgereckt einen Augenblick, zerbrach im Getöse und Gebrüll,
– herausgeschleudert aus dem europäischen Feld. Gautier
Fémin ist tot!

Wir aber schreiten aus! En avant! En avant! Wir umkreisen
die fünfzehn Fronten der europäischen Völker: Aviatiker,
kristalline Scheinwerfer, Säulen dröhnend im Sonnen-Aufgang!
Zerrissenste irdischste Dionyse, sammeln wir uns an den
enormen Städte-Pfeilern rasender Gewölbe Europas –: Hymne
geballt aus den Finsternissen des Dukla-Passes, den Ozean-
Schäumen des Skager-Rak, den Gasen von Loos, dem erdigen
Blut der Somme-Ufer und besudeltem Schutt des Do-berdo und
des Amselfeldes: – so wandeln wir, leuchtende Windhose, über
deine Ebenen, Europa! … … … Schon in den Metropolen baun
sich neue Barrikaden (… und wieder: die Untergrundbahnen
brechen herauf und sprühen empor! ein Bahnhof schwebt in der
Luft! …), überwallt von dem zehnfarbenen, firmamenthaften
Banner unendlich gewollter, gewollter Zukunft! … Wir werden
wiederkehren, Heimat Europas über uns, Heimat grüßend von
Pol zu Pol! Hallende Türme gotischer Kathedralen neigen sich,
die Glocken schwingen, und, leise, schwellend mehr und mehr,
hebt an endlich brausender Gesang, Gesang über verschüttetem
Tod und Leben!!

(Felix Stiemer in Freundschaft gewidmet)

MIRAMÉE
(PARIS)

Das Verhängnis hub an in einer gläsernen Sommernacht auf dem Boulevard Poissonniére. Eine Dame sank um im Lichtkreis einer Laterne; ich fing sie in meinen Armen auf. Es war Miramée. Ihr Kopf lag an meiner Schulter. Das Antlitz tauchte, einer Insel gleich, traumhaft und weich aus dem Äther ihres Haars. Eine seltsame Schönheit ruhte in ihm, als sie einen Augenblick lang die Augen öffnete und sie langsam wieder schloß. Es war, als sei der lange Boulevard feierlich mit diesem Blick in sie eingeflossen und hinter ihren seufzenden Lippen vergangen. Sie schmiegte den Kopf tiefer zu mir, ihre Hände umklammerten sanft meinen Arm, und sie erholte sich ein wenig. »Es geht Ihnen nicht gut, Madame«, sagte ich leise. Sie flüsterte: »Ach, ich hab zu viel gelitten!«

Ich rief einen Wagen an. Als ich beim Einsteigen half und ihre Schwere einen Augenblick lang trug, fühlte ich, wie eine große gemeinsame Welle durch uns beide schwebte und sich im Fluss der Bäume und Laternen verlor.

Der Boulevard schien sehr schmal und malte hektische Bilder an die fließenden Fenster unseres Autos. Miramée lag groß in den Polstern. Manchmal warf ein Fenster, einem

Scheinwerfer gleich, eine Kaskade von Licht auf ihren Schoß. Ihr blauseidenes Kleid glänzte auf. Unendlich hing ihr Blick an mir. Dann kam ein Augenblick, währenddessen ich deutlich begriff, daß ich sie früher schon einmal gesehen, gehalten, geliebt – geliebt haben mußte.

Wo sahn wir uns schon?

Miramée, in der Nacht trafen wir uns quer durch den schlimmen Schlaf der Weltstadt und durch die Nebel der Menschen, die des Nachts aufglimmen und durch die Straßen schreien ohne Stimme. *Schon verstricken uns gnadenlose Fäden.* Unsre Hände falten sich, und süß ist es, im Meer sich aufzulösen und durch die sieben Morgenröten zu hallen ohne Grenzen!

Dann waren wir in einem großen Hotel dicht bei der Madeleine, schattenhaft in einem gelben Zimmer. Ein Bett wuchs schwarz, war ein dröhnender Sarg. Der elektrische Kronleuchter, ein böses rotes Geschwür, neigte sich schwer darüber. Sie erzählte mir ihr ganzes Leben, das makabre Wüten ihres Schicksals, mit einer verlorenen Stimme, die die Wände entlang schluchzte.

Soll ich das Lied singen, das zu mir kam, dieses Lied, das sich um den Eiffelturm spannt und wirbelt in einem unsäglichen *vivace furioso?* ... das kreißte und Welten aufwarf von schluchzenden Dimensionen? – Apachen von Montmartre, Studenten des Quartier Latin, Amerikaner auf gewaltigen Schiffen und in schreienden Häusern, die des Abends Tausende von Menschen und Wasserfälle von Licht speien, erglühende Abende im Wald von Compiègne, fürchterliche Nächte in schmierigen und drohenden Hotels an den großen Boulevards, das Gleiten der Seine unter der Qual ihrer grauen Brücken, eine tiefe Liebe voll Angst und Not, steinerne Ärzte mit sachlichen Feststellungen, die feindseligen Betten der Salpêtrière, und, durch dies alles hindurch, im Hunger geträumt, die bestürzende Silhouette des schlanksten aller Türme über Paris im unbegreiflichen Glanz des Morgenhimmels: Silber und Blei, schimmernd und dumpf …

Ich lauschte, lauschte, und leise bildete sich in mir ihr kleines, unwirkliches Profil, wie es oft gewesen sein mußte auf der schwebenden Höhe in den weiten Falten der Sacré-Cœur-Kirche nach der Beichte. Miramée stieg hinab auf Paris, rein und golden ihr Schritt, eine süße Cirruswolke, die zu uns Menschen kam und verging, verging in Rauch und Schlamm.

Lang blieb ich noch entrückt und jenseits. Dann grinste sich das Hier wieder in mich ein. Ihr Leib lag bloß und weiß im Bett, *das mir wie ein endloses Meer schien, hallend und urhaft.* Eine bleiche Sonne quoll durch die Gardinen hüstelnd über die Dächer des Madeleine-Viertels herein. Koste ihre rechte Brust. Die linke lag böse zerfressen und geschwürig, braun und voll tückischen Lebens. Ihr armer Leib war eine Grotte von faulenden Massen, mühsam verklebt und verbunden. Das rechte Bein, schwarz von sich abschälender Haut, ragte wie ein verbrannter Pfahl in die Luft. Und all diese Stellen, auf die sich die furchtbare Krankheit gestürzt hatte, schillerten von einem gespenstischen Leben. Fast schien die Verwesung schon beginnen zu wollen, und je mehr sie fortschritt, um so mehr schien es mir, als ob ein neues Wesen da entstände, aus ihren Augenhöhlen kicherte und in den Zähnen hinter den toten, hochgezogenen Lippen lebte.

Eine sinnlose Angst faßte mich. Die Glocken begannen zu läuten, lange schleiften ihre wilden Töne über mich hin. Waren es nicht schwere Silben, die sie lallten, langsam und groß: »MI-RA-MÉE, MI-RA-MÉE«? – Paris stand auf und brüllte mich an. Ich stürzte wie wahnsinnig aus dem Hotel, Straßenkämpfe schienen mir zu toben, *die Untergrundbahnen brachen herauf und kamen empor, ein Bahnhof schwebte in der Luft.*

Ich rannte, ohne Hut, ohne Besinnung.

In einer Vorstadt hielt ich an, erschöpft auf einer Bank. Dann verließ mich das Bewußtsein. Als ich aufwachte, hatte man mich in eine nahe Schenke gebracht. Dort reichte man mir Schnaps. Die Pariser Arbeiter umstanden mich in ihren blauen Blusen und diskutierten eifrig. Draußen, auf dem Boulevard Ornano, zitterte die Sonne, Spatzen piepsten, und vom Hof her kam das leise Singen eines kleinen unbewußten Dienstmädchens:

»C'est une belle gosse,
mais une sale rosse,
on ne devrait jamais l'approcher.
O quelle torture
que l'on endure,
quand on a le malheur de l'aimer!«

Ich aber ging, weiße Rosen in der Hand, langsam und leicht den Boulevard Ornano entlang, aus Paris hinaus, in die uferlosen Felder.

KABARETT

Das Kabarett hat einen riesenhaften Namen. Wie ein
Berliner Warenhaus oder ein New-Yorker Wolkenkratzer.
Auch der Duft der Pariser Untergrundbahn ist mir da, wenn
ich ihn höre: »*Metropol-Bierpalast*«. Darum ging ich hin,
mit ihr, der Sehr-Schönen, Sehr-Lieben. Da es noch früh
war, bekamen wir den wunderschönsten Platz und waren
glücklich. Die Musiker lagen vereinzelt, unvollzählig auf
dem Podium herum wie Wachsfiguren; sie waren noch nicht
in Betrieb gesetzt. Plötzlich verdunkelte mir der Bauch des
Oberkellners alle Aussicht, so daß ich in Schrecken und
Aufregung geriet und nach einem Schutzmann spähte; denn
ich hielt das für nicht erlaubt. Der aber stand unbekümmert
streng an einer Türe; wußte, daß sein Dasein so mächtig
war, daß er auch hätte abwesend sein können und wäre doch
Herr geblieben im Sturm der Antlitze, Gläser und Lichter.
Oft schwebten Wesen vorbei in weiten weißen oder zart
hellfarbenen Blusen, die sich wie Segel im Winde blähten.
Ich hielt sie für himmlische Fledermäuse, und ihre Augen
schauten sehr klug aus dem Schmelz der Haare hervor. Das
ganze Innere des Kabaretts war japanisch ausstaffiert und
hieß »Eine Nacht im Reich des Mikado«. An die Wände
waren große Bilder mit japanischen Männern und Frauen

gespannt, die dasaßen oder -standen und sich ansahen, als wollten sie in der nächsten Minute unzüchtige Handlungen begehen. In der Nähe des Ausgangs taten sie es auch wirklich, aber das bemerkte ich erst beim Fortgehen. Die Decke war eine Wolke von Papierlaternen und Lampions. Einige drehten sich fortwährend um sich selbst, wie von einem Uhrwerk getrieben. Später schrieb ich jede süße Folge der Orchestermusik *ihrer* Bewegung zu und war so den ganzen Abend über aufrichtig dankbar gegen diese Papierlampen, zu denen man emporblicken konnte wie zu Göttern.

Wir tranken Bier. Das leise Vorübergleiten der weißen Fledermäuse dauerte an. Auf einmal barst das Orchester in einem brillanten Akkord. Der Dirigent, im lila Frack, schwamm gewaltig oben auf. Die Kontrabässe der Zweiten Ungarischen Rhapsodie zogen mächtige Furchen in die Menschenmenge. Am Nebentisch wurde Wein getrunken; es klirrte Geld, und man stieß mit den Gläsern an, während oben im Orchester Frisca mit ihrem Tanzen den armen Lassan verrückt machte. Ich war sehr froh, als es dann endlich zum Koitus kam: *tempo giusto*, ratatáh dadatatáh …

Dann war eine kleine Pause, während der das Gespräch der Besucher wie ein Mückenschwarm an der japanischen Decke hing. Die Musiker räumten überraschend schnell das Podium und verzogen sich ganz in seinen Hintergrund. Der schneeweiße Scheinwerfer blitzte auf und bespie sie mit unerbittlicher Beleuchtung. Ich schloß sanft die Augen, um abzuwarten, bis das Licht Kraft genug gesammelt haben würde, eine Person auf die Bühne zu materialisieren. Als ich wieder aufsah, stand dort ein Mädchen im kurzen Kinderkleidchen, das den Eindruck einer Zehnjährigen erwecken sollte, und schrie mit Rohfleischstimme ein Lied über die Schlamperei in Wien. Jedes Wort war ein Spucknapf, jede Geste gewerbsmäßige Unzucht. Sie verschwand schnell, denn ich entzog ihr meine Projektionsfläche.

Als ich mich zurücksetzen wollte, tauchte ich unvermutet mit den Blicken in das Décolletée einer Dame, die nahebei saß. Dort blieb ich liegen bis zur nächsten Nummer.

Das war eine gigantische Negerin mit ungeheurem, gepanzertem Brustkorb. Sie wuchs auf die Bühne wie ein Turm. Der Kapellmeister glitzerte mit seinen Brillanten und schillerte mit dem Frack. Sie hatte ein feuerrotes Schleppkleid an, und ihre Augen waren Büsche im Urwald. Sie sang mit strahlendem Gebiß und majestätischem Blick ein englisches Lied, während ihr Kinn bulldogghaft hin- und herschwappte. Sie trat als Stimmphänomen auf; ihre Stimme war wie geschmolzener Stahl im Hochofenausfluß; bei den piano-Stellen kreiste sie über uns wie ein tropischer Sternenhimmel. Sie bekam viel Applaus; selbst meine Kleine war erschüttert und klatschte. Dann sang sie ein amerikanisches Tanzlied, tanzte aber nicht beim Refrain, sondern deutete im synkopierten Zucken der Unterarme und Knöchel den Tanz nur an, der vielleicht alle Saloons der *Bowery* bewegt. Mein Herz hüpfte mit.

Dann war sie fort. Ich sah sie durch die Menge schreiten, beifallumplätschert. Sie entfernte sich, und ihr Kleid, feuerrot und immer dunkler werdend, schleppte nach. Und plötzlich kam mir ein dämmerndes Gefühl, Ahnung von Abschied, und Gesichter tauchten mir auf, die lange in meiner Seele gelegen hatten. Ich klammerte mich innerlich an die Frau neben mir, die ich liebte, und wollte einen Augenblick lang fort. Doch schon gab die Musik eine Einlage.

Es war sehr lustig. Der Kapellmeister ulkte mit dem Taktstock, und das Publikum amüsierte sich sehr. In mir war ein Wirbel. Ich war ganz nahe bei der Frau neben mir, die ich liebte. Sie redete, ich hörte zu. Manchmal sprach auch ich, doch fiel mir nie ein, das zu sagen, was eigentlich in mir war. Eine neue Reihe der weißen Engel floß still vorbei; sie gingen in die Bar. Ich war weit fort, die Zeit verfloß wohl. Als ich einmal auf das Podium sah, erblickte ich einen drolligen Neger mit einer Baßklarinette. Auf der grölte er: *»Mariette, ma midinette«* ... Seine Partnerin verbot ihm das, er tat es aber immer wieder. Sie stellte ein *American girl* vor und hatte sehr wenig an. Ihre starken und festen Brüste, über die sich das Kleid straffte, wälzten sich mir um den Kopf. Ich dachte, das Kleid würde zerreißen, aber das geschah nicht.

Ein Humorist kam, sang, erzählte, machte Kapriolen. Wir lachten beide sehr. Dann gingen wir. Unter der Tür schillerte der Kapellmeister noch einmal gewaltig auf; aber die japanischen Bilder, die schon zu großer Unzucht übergegangen waren, ließen uns links liegen. Die Lampions tanzten, die Musik schrie, die Blusen leuchteten. – Was blieb, war das Gesicht der Garderobefrau, arm, fern, nüchtern und eindringlich. *War sie es, die ich dann später in den Armen hielt, in der heißen, uferlosen Nacht?*

NOCTURNE
(KÖLN)

Ich komme am Dom vorbei. Der steht da – unersättlich, mit der großen in die Nacht hineingreifenden Gebärde …

Kleine weiche Kokotten stehen im Schatten der Häuser und haben jenes mir ach so bekannte Zucken um den Mund, wenn ein großer gedunsener Mann auf sie zutappt und mit breiten Froschfingern ihre kleine Brust betastet.

Und ich stehe auf dem Bahnhof.

Da liegt der braune Zug in den Gleisen, der nachts seine Not von London über Ostende, Berlin und Warschau nach Moskau heult, atmend wie ein gepeinigtes Tier.

Und ich weiß: –

Um diese Zeit sinken schwere Wolken von Schnee tief in die kanadischen Wälder;

um diese Zeit wälzt sich ein kranker, müder Krake auf dem Meeresgrund dem Tode zu;

um diese Zeit bröckelt wieder eine zermorschte Landschaft von dem greisen Monde ab. –

Und ich weiß: –

Ich empfinde das alles: das tiefe Elend, in dem ich liege, das helle Glück, zu dem ich fliege in anderen Stunden;

in mir ist die Angst des Bibers; der Hunger des Känguruhs, das unter südlichen Sternen einsam auf flüsternden Steppen springt; meine Seele ist ein Zwinger voll wilder Tiere, voll lauernder, boshafter Affen und nagender Hyänen;

und ich bin machtlos, arm; ich falle vor ihr nieder wie ein nackter Wilder, der im heißen Dunst und Dunkel brütender Sümpfe die Kugelblitze um den Kilima-Ndscharo rollen hört; –

und doch weine ich und lache und singe mit zersprungenen Lippen;

und mein Herz glüht wie eine Perle, und meine Augen sind Diamanten: –

Meine Welt! Meine tanzende, große Welt!

ANKUNFT

(28. JULI 1914)

Der dumpfe Bahnhof in der Sommernacht
brüllt wie ein Tier, und in der weiten Halle
stehn tausend Menschen, stumm und dunkel alle
und in sich zu, *als gingen sie zur Schlacht.*

Und wie die Züge mit gewältztem Schalle
eindringen in des bösen Leibes Pracht,
ist ein schwarze Sonne aufgewacht
und hängt am Himmel, nah, als ob sie falle.

– Und in mir taumelt schwer und ungeschlacht
furchtbare Kälte auf! – spannt ihre Kralle
wie eine Fledermaus vors Licht; entfacht

das Dunkel neu zu grenzenlosem Wall.
Und platzend quillt mein Herz aus seinem Schacht, –
– wird dröhnend gross, wird zum Lawinen-Ball.

GEBET IM KRIEG

Der du brausest in Kanonen-
Aufruhr, und im wirren Glanze
manchmal zeigst ein huschendes Gesicht;

Gast bei Leichnamen, die thronen
stumm am Hügel, fern vom Tanze,
wirr verhauchend klagend Licht;

der du wanderst in den Gräben,
ohne Ziel, verweint und lungernd,
schleichst um Feuer in erstickter Qual:

Gib uns, blass in tierisch totem Leben,
war wir sehnen, dumpf und hungernd;
zeig uns deiner Hände glühend Mal!

Oft gekreuzigt sind wir und sehr bitter
Mit verfluchtem Essig-Schwamm getränkt;
regungslos im Bajonetten-Gitter
unsre Leiber blutig eingezwängt.

Heb dich auf im tosenden Gewitter,
das ob unsern leeren Hirnen hängt
Mach uns frei, du: Friedenfürst und Ritter,

Toten-Wecker! Himmlisches Geschenk!!

(Für René Schickele)

MAGISCHER GESANG

Ich bin ein Mensch – ich fürchte mich.
Die schwarzen Wolken fürchte ich,
sie: eisern schallend an des Himmels totem Rand!
Und Häusermauern scheue ich,
Die stummen Türen bangen mich;
blinzelnde Klinke dran, wie schicksalvoll berührt sie meine
        Hand!

Auf graue Schauer-Erde fürchterlich
gebannt, und unter kalten Gottes Hieb und Mörder-Stich
– ein Mensch!, welch Schatten grossen, unabwendbaren
        Geschehens!
Ich fürchte mich, ich ängste mich,
gebaut, gelenkt nach Rätselwort und magischem Strich,
mächtig umkreist von Stern und Sturm und unfassbarem
        Einmaleins!

Im Blitz der nahen Sonne morgendlich,
und in des ahnungsvollen Herzens tiefem Abendlicht
erkenn ich mich und dich, uns alle, die wir qualvoll sind!
Was uns von Urbeginn beschlich,
das Wesen, Raubtier – Gott!, Entsetzen fühle ich!

Wie wir gefangen sind, verscharrt und zugedeckt von Nacht
      und Wind!

Ich fühle, schaue! – Mensch bin ich.
Vor meinem Schauen fürcht ich mich;
o Blutes Beben unter Sternen! o des Herzens grosser Blick!
Meins Schritt, mein Laut, mein tiefer Schlaf und Atem und
      des Pulses Klang.
Mein Weib, mein Kind. O Schweigen! O der Erde grosser,
      unhörbarer Gang!
Ich bin ein Mensch. Ich fürchte nicht! Ich liebe das Geschick!

(Köln, 2.7.21, abends 18 Uhr)

NACHT UND TRAUM

Wir haben alle Städte fremd durchquert,
und Ferne strahlt aus unsrem Paletot.
Die Häuser brennen fahl in unsrer Haut.
Baum und Laternen sind ein Dorn-Geflecht
um unser stern-besätes blaues Hirn.

Die grosse Krankheit fast uns wütend an,
legt grenzenlosen Raum in unsre Brust;
und um die Kerze wirbelnd fieber-toll
wirft sie uns auf die Betten, leer und tot.

Doch draussen qualmt die fürchterliche Nacht!
Der Erde Drehen dröhnt durch sie hindurch.
Auf Ozeanen taumeln hilflos-starr
die Schiffe wie ein steif-gewordnes Aas,

voll Menschen, ihrer Brüder eingedenk,
in riesenhaften Häusern auf dem Land,
das in der gnadenlosen Sonne brennt
wie ein Geschwür und immer böser schwärt. —

Zu dieser Stunde blüht wohl in Bedrlin
der Hochbahn lichte Blume sanft empor;
voll Menschen, ihre Brüder eingedenk,
die nun am Kap der Guten Hoffnung sind
und in der Tafelberge Mondes-Blau
Fliegende Hunde und Hyänen sehn.

Schwimmende Städte auf dem Hoang-ho:
Chinesen strudeln in Myriaden nach.
Ein dunkler Stern ist unsrer Erde nah.
Der Fluss kehrt um und wendet sich bergauf.

Wir alle, alle treiben in dem Fluss.
Erkennen wir uns nicht durch Flut und Tang?
Im Negermaul? Im Schopf des roten Manns? –
– Und schaun uns nicht von den Planeten an
Ferhrnrohe, ihrer Brüder eingedenk? –

Verwesen wir? Die Nacht ist immer da!
Süss sinken wir in namenlosen Samt.
Auf Firsten irren unsre Schatten schon.
Ans Fenster klopft ein sinnlos-grauer Tag.

Der Mond, das gelbe Auge, stiert uns zu
und wander wie ein Raubtier hin und her;
die Menschen sind hypnotisch ihm verstrickt
und hängen aus den Schloten leichenhaft.

Durch unsre toten Leiber treibt Gerank
von einer Frau, die unsre Seele hält.

Das stumme Bett steht in der Strasse still,
und trübe Menschen sagen »guten Tag«.
Mein toter Vater schwebt zu mir heran:
er gibt mit Geld, er hat mich lieb und lacht;
doch meine Mutter sitzt verdrossen hart,
versteht mich nicht und schwindet im Asphalt.

Durch tausend Sphären gross in Blau und Gold
schwingt *Gott der Herr* sich in mein Erden-Herz;
sein Rückgrat ist der Erde angeschmiegt
und schmerzt, und seine Augen sind sehr krank.

Geträumte Bilder fliehen mit Geschrei.
Zahnlos dampft eines Weibes brauner Mund;
jahrtausend-alt und milde schwankend gehn
Kamele über ihre Wüsten-Stirn.

Schon mündet gross der Nil in unser Herz.
Nun sind wir Meer, wir Sand, wir Nebel-Stern.
Erde geht fort; dort schwebt der bleiche Ball.
Und wir sind Stoff und Äther. Wer formt uns?

(Meinem totem Vater)

ENDE

Ich habe meinen Traum versenkt, ein letztes Mal mein Blut
       geküsst,
– ich zwischen Dunkelheiten und den schwarzen Feuern
       Schreitender.
Mein haupt is schwer, und tief berauscht mein Herz.

Ein Wald, ein Singe-Wald erfror; lautlos versank ein helles
       Schiff.
Die Vögel sterben, und das Eis kriecht in die Zimmer, in die
       Brust.
Und keine Sonne scheint, kein Stern! – die Himmel starren
       tot. –

Wie ist mir kalt! Mein Weib is fern, ich kenne kaum
das Antlitz meiner Kinder mehr. Die Locke, die ich lange trug,
– ein Heiligtum- ist starr und fremd.

– So würg ich denn mein leeres Herz, das mir Gespenster
       plünderten.
Ich schliess das Auge. Meine Stirn neig ich in tiefe letzte
       Nacht.

Sie wird mir kalte Freundin sein, wie auf den Strassen Hur
        und Hund,
um Windes-Ecken streichend, – eine letzte milde Trösterin …

»KOMM, HOLDER SCHNEE!«

Komm, holder Schnee! Verschütte dies schwere Herz!
Mit deiner Gnade zaubre die Träne starr,
so aus der ewigen Quelle rinnet,
täglich geboren, geliebt noch immer.

O gib, dass mir aus dieser verlorenen Qual,
der bittern, werde das grosse, das ernste Grab,
darin ich mich zur Ruhe finde:
weinende, liebend erlöste Seele.

Geschrieben am 10. März, 1925, abends um halb 7

ALSO IN THIS SERIES

Carl Einstein, *Negro Sculpture*,
translated by Patrick Healy (print, 2016 – ebook, 2014).

Carl Einstein, *Bebuquin, or the Dilettantes of the Miracle*,
translated by Patrick Healy (print 2017).

Karl Kraus, *The Last Days of Mankind: A Tragedy in Five Acts*,
translated by Patrick Healy (print and ebook 2016).

Karl Kraus, *In These Great Times: Selected Writings*,
translated by Patrick Healy (print, 2017 – ebook, 2014).

Else Lasker-Schüler, *My Heart: A Novel of Love*,
translated by Sheldon Gilman and Robert Levine
(print and ebook, 2016).

Max Raphael, *The Invention of Expressionism: Critical
Writings 1910-1913*, translated by Patrick Healy (print 2017).

IN PREPARATION

Albert Ehrenstein, *Tubutsch*,
translated by Gijs van Koningsveld.

www.ingramcontent.com/pod-product-compliance
Lightning Source LLC
Chambersburg PA
CBHW020642250626
47154CB00008B/2774